The Year of the Sawdust Man

A. LaFaye

ALADDIN PAPERBACKS

*Because no book is written by the author alone, I'd like to thank
God for making me a writer. I'd also like to thank Brett Singer,
James Newcomb, Thomas Russell, George Nicholson, David Gale,
Alix Reid, and Michael Conathan for helping me shape
this book into its present form.*

*This book is dedicated to Allyson—
A daughter who knows the trials of motherhood*

First Aladdin Paperbacks edition October 1999

Copyright © 1998 by Alexandria LaFaye

Aladdin Paperbacks
An imprint of Simon & Schuster Children's Publishing Division
1230 Avenue of the Americas, New York, NY 10020

Book design by Steve Scott
The text of this book is set in Granjon.
Printed and bound in the United States of America
4 6 8 10 9 7 5 3

The Library of Congress has cataloged the hardcover edition as follows:
LaFaye, A.
The year of the sawdust man / A. LaFaye.
p.   cm.
Summary: In 1934, when her mother leaves her and her father,
eleven-year-old Nissa tries to cope with the gossip of her small Louisiana
town and the changes in her own life.
ISBN 0-689-81513-1 (hc.)
[1. Mothers and daughters—Fiction. 2. Divorce—Fiction. 3. Remarraige—Fiction.
4. Louisiana—Fiction.] I. Title. PZ7.L1413Ye 1998   [Fic]—dc21
97-14501   CIP   AC
0-689-83106-4 (pbk.)

Contents

Fall Cleaning in May

I KNEW EVERY INCH OF MAMA'S ROOM. WE SPENT OUR DAYS there ever since we moved to that airy house on Main Street—cutting paper dolls from magazine advertisements or acting out plays from the books we'd read. Mama loved the models in the *Ladies' Home Journal* because they placed their hands on their hips, so she could cut them out easily and change their clothes with dresses we drew and colored ourselves. For our plays, we made costumes out of the laundry Mama cleaned for our neighbors. Mama enjoyed play-acting more than cleaning clothes. We spent so much time in that breezy room overlooking Minkie's Mercantile, I knew every ring of dust, every pierced earring, every piece of handmade clothing she owned.

I went into her room after school. It was Friday, May the seventh. We only had a few weeks left of school. I was looking forward to spending my days with Mama again. I went in to tell Mama the mercantile was buzzing with the news that the postmistress, Miss Roubidoux, was caught reading other people's mail again. The windows were open in Mama's room and there was the faint smell of melting wax, but no sign of Mama.

I went to the hall and called her name, but there was no answer. Sometimes Mama had a mind to ignore me, so I went out to the garden to find her. It was the roses that told me she'd gone. She kept a bed of purple roses and every single bush was bare. Mama had gone through and cut away each flower. The stems themselves cluttered the ground around the bushes. She'd harvested the petals. I'd seen her do it in the fall when there was threat of a frost. I ran back in the house hoping I'd see a newspaper spread out over the counter, covered with hundreds of rose petals the shade of grape sour balls.

The counters were empty and clean. I noticed that the floors in the hallway were scrubbed to a shine. The banister going upstairs was polished and glossy smooth under my hand. I could see the shine in the wood and smell the lemon oil. The curtains in the window on the landing smelled of soap. Mama had done her fall cleaning in May. Mama didn't like cleaning. She only did it when she had to, so the only reason she'd do her fall cleaning early was if she didn't plan on being around come fall.

I checked the hall closet to be sure. Mama's brown leather suitcase with the brass clasps was gone. I told myself she'd only gone away for a month or so, maybe to see Aunt Sarah again. She'd gone up to Virginia the winter before, after a bad bout with the flu, and come back for Christmas ready to take on the entire town of Harper, Louisiana, in the game of their choosing.

I went back to her room to see what she'd taken, trying to prove she'd be back soon. Sitting at her vanity, I could see that she'd taken her silver hairbrush and her curlers, but her bottles of perfume and the box of pink talcum powder were still there. I checked her drawers. She'd left behind her wool sweater and the long underwear Papa had bought her for our trip to Buffalo to buy a printing press for Papa's boss. She'd taken the blue blouse with the glass buttons and the gray skirt Grandma Dee had sent for her birthday. The bottom drawer was empty and that made no sense. Baby Benjamin's clothes were usually in there. Ben was the baby boy Mama had when we lived on the farm by the Amite River. He was born small, then he got real sick before he was old enough to walk. He died of pneumonia when he was nine months and thirteen days old. We buried him in a coffin made of cherry wood under the shade of a bald cypress tree in the cemetery above Sutton's Creek, but Mama kept some of his clothes. He had a pair of red overalls with blue bears stitched over the knees and three little white T-shirts made out of a cotton so soft it felt like the fur of a kitten. Mama kept the clothes tucked away in a drawer with hearts carved out of cedar to keep them smelling fresh and safe from moths. Mama always said she kept the clothes for the next baby to come along, but none ever did.

Why would she take the baby clothes with her? Was she going to have a new baby? Was she really just going off to have her baby in one of those fancy hospitals where they have an entire wing just for women having babies?

I ran to the closet to see if she'd taken her housecoat. Mama always said any self-respecting woman would have a silk robe just in case she had to be in the hospital and other people were allowed to see her in her pajamas. Her housecoat was there, but the floral pink Sunday dress with the real pearls holding together the shoulder gathers was gone. What was still there scared me all the more. She'd left behind her favorite dress—the one with the gauzy violet fabric that made a tiny crunch like sand when you rubbed it together between your fingers. It didn't make any sense. I wanted to run over to the newspaper office to ask Papa where she was, but I knew he wouldn't know. She'd left while we were gone from the house and there was no note; Mama didn't want us to know where she'd gone.

I sat on Mama's bed, which smelled of lilac oil, trying to decide if I should cry. I knew she was gone, but I felt hollow inside—not sad, just hollow. I was staring at nothing in particular, unable to shuffle my thoughts together; then I noticed the picture of me and Papa in the old Model T was missing. We looked good in the front seat. He'd let me wear his driving cap with the goggles on the bill. I liked the way Papa was smiling because his eyes wrinkled up as if they were smiling, too. He was gripping the steering wheel so you could see his wedding ring. Remembering how Papa's ring sparkled in the sun, I wondered if maybe Mama would see the ring and think how bad it was to leave her husband, but I knew it wouldn't make her come back.

There was no need to take a picture of us along if she expected to see us soon, so I figured she was never coming back. I sat there thinking to myself that Mama had left for good, yet no tears came.

Papa came home and found me sitting there, staring. "Where's your mother?" he asked, leaning into the room. Then he called out for her, "Heirah?"

"She's gone," I whispered.

Papa knew Mama well enough to know "gone" didn't mean she was out picking berries along Sutton's Creek. Mama had threatened to leave before. Once, when I was little, she'd even packed all her things in a trunk, then dragged it to the bus stop. Papa knew what "gone" really meant. He stepped into the room and took a few deep breaths. "How do you know?"

"No suitcase, no Sunday dress, no silver brush, and she took Benjamin's clothes. Papa, why would she take the baby clothes?"

His body went stiff. He straightened out his back and clenched his fists. "Go ring Grandma Dee."

"What are you going to do?" I asked, standing up.

"Just ring your grandmother."

"Yes, Papa." I ran downstairs and crossed Main Street to use the phone in Minkie's Mercantile. The Minkies let us use their phone on account of all the help Papa gave them. He stocked the store every Saturday after Mr. Minkie fell out of his apple tree and hurt his back.

"What's the hurry, Nissa?" Mr. Minkie asked as I came in.

"I have to call Grandma Dee."

"Calling Mississippi in the middle of the day? It must be some real big news brewing," Mrs. Minkie said from the dry-goods counter. She was fishing for gossip, as usual.

"Grandma doesn't like to be dragged all the way into town after dark," I said, to cut Mrs. Minkie's fishing line before she tried to bait me with a piece of candy.

"All right." Mr. Minkie waved toward the phone booth by the fabric counter. "Call now before the train comes through."

I rushed into the phone booth, slammed the door to keep my conversation away from Mrs. Minkie's nosy ears, then cranked it up to put a charge through to Becky at the switchboard. She connected me to the lady in Buellah. I never remember her name, but she always says Louisiana with a "wheezy" in the middle, so that's what I call her. While I waited for Wheezy to fetch Grandma Dee from the sewing shop, I picked at the newspaper lining the wall. I ripped a corner away. An ugly old headline stared out at me, shouting "Happy New Year 1933!" in stiff, black letters. My year wasn't too darn happy with Mama leaving. That old newspaper could just swallow the whole year and spit it out for all I cared.

I heard the strangled goose sound of Papa starting up the Model T. He was going to search for Mama. I prayed he'd find her for his sake as well as mine. I knew he loved her enough to drive all the way to Chicago to buy her the bare roots for her purple roses.

Still, I knew he wouldn't find her. Mama could get lost in a gust of wind. She'd be sitting at the table decorating a carrot cake with raisins, then a wind would come along and shake the curtains. Mama would tilt her head, then lift her chin into the wind and she'd stare off into another time and place. It didn't pay to ask where she'd gone. I'd pull on her sleeve asking her to talk to me, but she'd keep right on staring into that other place where I couldn't go. When Mama left, she went where no one could find her.

There was the clip-clop of footsteps echoing over the phone line, then Grandma Dee shouted, "Hello?" She never did figure out that she didn't have to yell to be heard over the telephone.

"Mama's gone, Grandma Dee. Mama's gone." I didn't have to identify myself. I was her only grandchild.

"Holy prayers. When did she leave?"

"Today!"

"No idea where she went?"

"No. She just took her things and a picture of me and Papa and disappeared."

"That girl. Don't you worry, Nissa, your mama didn't leave you. She'll be back."

"Then why'd she take a picture of me and Papa?"

"Because she loves you and she wants you with her no matter where she goes, but she'll be back. You just wait and see."

I wanted to believe Grandma Dee, but Mama always said grandmas are bound to lie if it'll make you feel better. And Mama was most often right. She wasn't coming back, so I was ready to go find her. No one knew Mama better than me. I could track her down.

I had my suitcase open on the bed and I was dropping in a pile of shirts when Papa came home. He came running up the steps. He took them two or three at a time, looking like he was jumping from rock to rock in Sutton's Creek. He yelled, "Neesay!"

He calls me Neesay. My name's Nissa after Papa's mama who died before their family left Norway. Papa calls me Neesay and I wonder if it's what Grandpa Knut called Grandma Nissa before she died. I can't ask him. Grandpa doesn't speak English and he lives in Minnesota. I wish I could meet him someday. I'd like to know more about Grandma seeing as how I'm named after her, and all. Papa doesn't remember much about her because he was only five when she died, but he told me once that she used to fry muffins on a skillet like pancakes and drop the batter just right, so the muffins were shaped like little people when they were done.

Papa came into my room, holding a jar. "Look what I've brought you."

He'd brought me a treat from the mercantile. He'd gone off to find Mama and come back with something to eat. What was he thinking?

It was Mrs. Minkie's grapes preserved in their own juices. "Eyeballs in spit," as Mama called them. I loved the smooth feeling of their skins on my tongue and the sweet gush of their fruit when I pressed them against the roof of my mouth. Papa was all smiles, making the hairs he'd missed under his chin stick out, trying to make it seem like things were just fine now that I had my grapes. Then he saw my suitcase. "What's this?"

"I'm going to find Mama," I said, putting my white straw Easter hat on so the blue ribbons hung down to my shoulders. Mama always said to wear hats in the sun so your eyes won't go bad from squinting.

Papa set the grapes down on my dresser, then put his hand on my shoulder, saying, "Leave that suitcase and come with me."

I followed Papa to Mama's room. Mama had her own bedroom because women have just as much right to their own room as men do and Papa had his den. We sat in the window seat where Mama liked to read. Papa held out his hand and I hooked my fingers between his. His hands were as rough as raw wood on his palms and fingertips, but the skin between his fingers was as smooth as Mama's cheeks.

"Mama didn't leave you, Nissa. She left me."

"We live together."

Papa closed his eyes. "She didn't want to live with me anymore."

"Then why not take me?"

"Would you be happy if she had?"

"No." I didn't want to go off with Mama if it meant leaving Papa. I wanted Mama in the window seat reading Winnie-the-Pooh out loud, like she did on Sunday nights, with Papa and me at her feet. I liked having Papa's laughter blowing through my hair as I sat on his lap. Mama did such a great Piglet voice; even my best friend, Mary Carroll, came over to hear her squeal on occasion. I picked at the dirt under Papa's nail, then asked, "Why didn't she want to live with you anymore?"

"Nissa," Papa shook our hands. "You know how mad you get when you're trying to put all the pieces of a puzzle together and they just don't fit?"

I'd been known to send the pieces of a puzzle flying if I couldn't solve it. "Yeah."

"Well, sometimes people's minds get like that. You know what you want and what you have, but you just can't fit them all together in a way that makes you happy."

Sometimes Papa tried too hard to make things easy for me to understand and made no sense whatsoever. "I don't follow you."

He sighed. "Your mama has things here in Harper that she loves, like you and her garden, but there are other things

Fall Cleaning in May 9

she wants that aren't here in Harper, so she's going after them."

"Without us?"

"Yes, but it's not because she doesn't love you."

"Does she love *you*?"

Papa bowed his head. "She's mad at me for not giving her the things she wanted."

"Why didn't you?"

"I tried, but there are some things you can't just go out and get. It isn't that easy."

"What does she want?"

"Friends she can go to when she needs to talk and the freedom to do whatever she wants." Papa looked down at me. I could tell by the heavy look in his eyes that there was more he wasn't telling me.

"I know people here don't like Mama, but we do. We're her friends. We let her do what she wants."

Papa smiled just a little. "We certainly do, but I suppose we weren't enough."

I wanted to cry. I couldn't see how Mama would ever dream that leaving us could make her happy. Papa and I would do anything for Mama. Papa'd even walk her to anywhere she wanted to go—even if it was the tip of Argentina. Unless, well, maybe Papa didn't love her anymore. Maybe he was mad at her for leaving.

"You still love Mama?" I asked.

He lifted my hand up and kissed it. "I love you."

"And Mama?"

"Yes, and Mama."

Dragons and Flies

Sitting on a window seat in my room, I stared at Mama's garden down below, hoping I could cry. Tears wash your soul clean. That's what Papa told me. They shrink your pain down to size, he says. The problem was I didn't feel any pain. Mama was gone, maybe even for good, and all I could do was sit here and stare at the stems she'd cut to the quick and left for the heat to devour.

Mama used to say Louisiana heat comes from a dragon who's so large she could scratch her eyebrows on a cloud. That scaly creature's hunkered down in a huge swamp somewhere, breathing fire in her sleep. That old fire turns the water to steam which floats across Louisiana and makes us all sweat until our minds start to melt. I told myself that was the problem. It was too darn hot. When evening came and things cooled off maybe my thoughts would get up and move around again—then I'd really be able to believe Mama was gone. Then I'd cry. I'd cry so hard, I'd warp the wood beneath my feet with water.

Truth was it doesn't get all that hot in the early part of May. But I kept blaming my silence on the heat. The cicadas screamed and I wished I could do the same. The birds picked their way through Mama's dying flowers looking for bits of this and that for their nests. I was thinking how fine it would be to have rose petals as purple as the potbelly of an eggplant lining a baby's bed. Them little birdies would have it made. It was too bad that Mama had taken the petals with her.

I heard Papa shuffling about in the kitchen down below. He was probably making sandwiches with dill pickles and mustard. He never made much else. I already had one of my own. I could taste the sour sting of pickles in the back of my mouth, but it just sat there on the windowsill, the holes in the bread staring up at me like a hundred eyes, asking, "Why aren't you crying, Nissa Bergen?"

I told myself, "Just let them tears come."

They didn't. I heard Papa come upstairs one step at a time, then go into his study across the hall. I begin to wonder, would Papa cry? Was he sitting behind his desk bawling over his sandwich? I figured I'd be able to hear him from where I sat. When Baby Benjamin died, I could hear Papa crying clear on the other side of the house.

We were in the old house on Wakefield Road. Mama and Papa had the same room back then. Mama and I were sleeping in their bed. I had slept with my head on her chest, so I could hear her heart beat and know she wouldn't leave me in her sleep like little Bennie did. It'd gotten real cool that night, like the dragon was walking the earth instead of hunkering down in her swamp to make some steam. Maybe she was mourning my baby brother as well. I'd felt all warm where Mama and I touched, but my back felt so cold. I'd wanted Papa to be there like he was on Sunday mornings when I'd crawled into bed with Mama and him. We'd sleep all snuggled up like possums in their mama's pocket. After Bennie was born, he had slept under Mama's arm at the edge of the bed with a pile of pillows on the floor below. I slept between Mama and Papa.

I'd prayed for Papa to come as I fell asleep, but when I woke up it was dark enough for the moon to turn Mama's white curtains into silver and he wasn't there. At first, I heard a sound that made me think Bennie had the hiccups. I was about to wake Mama when I realized Bennie was gone. Gone for good. I'd started to cry all over again. When I heard the herk and the jerk of my own tears I knew that sound I'd heard was crying. Papa was crying.

I got out of bed and followed the sound. As I got closer, it sounded like glass being broken inside of a fabric sack—over and over until all that was left were tiny unbreakable pieces. Papa was curled up on the couch, his face buried in the baby blanket he clutched in his hands. For a second, I couldn't go to him. It hurt too much to even see him all bent up and shaking. I was scared. Then Papa saw me. He sat up, closed his eyes in silence, then looked at me. Smiling, he said, "Come to me, Neesay."

He held his hand out, but when I came close and put my hand up for him to take, he took all of me instead. He pulled me up onto the couch and we curled up together and cried. It was like we melted together and bawled until we fell asleep. Next morning, I woke up in Papa's arms and it felt like I was a baby in a little nest and everything would be fine.

* * *

I wanted that feeling again, but I felt so darn guilty that I couldn't even cry. I hadn't shed one tear. Was I mad? Mama had left without so much as a note. Was I sad? She was my best friend in the world. Was I scared? I had no idea where Mama'd run off to. Anything could happen to her.

The truth was, I didn't feel any of those things. I was empty. There was nothing inside me but dead air. I pushed my sandwich off the sill and watched the pickles fall out of the bread and wiggle and turn as they fell into the garden below. I thought maybe I'd like to fly that way for a second or two. I imagined landing softly in the bed of Mama's roses, then I remembered—the rosebushes were nothing but thorns now and I'd get all cut up.

I heard the creak of Papa's chair, but I never heard him cry. I went across the hall and stood in front of the door, hoping I'd find a way to open it. It was only a few feet away, but I couldn't make myself step over to it and turn the knob. I heard the creak of a floorboard at the front of the house. There was a spark in my chest. Mama was back, I thought, but when I looked down the hall, the wind blew and made the floors whisper back, so I knew it wasn't her.

When I turned back to Papa's door, he was standing there looking down at me. He had a smile on his face. I couldn't believe it. Mama was gone and he looked like he'd just caught a giant catfish for supper.

"You're as stuck as I am, aren't you, Nissa?"

"Stuck?"

Papa sat on the floor, then lay down to stare at the ceiling. I thought he'd gone crazy flopping down there in the hall like a dog. He patted his flat tummy, saying, "It's like my heart's stuck. It won't go anywhere. I can't scream. I can't cry. I'm just stuck."

I don't know how I got there, but I found myself lying crossways, with my elbows on Papa's chest, saying, "Me too."

"Remember the time your mama got the idea she'd paint the house?" Papa asked.

We giggled seeing Mama standing on the ladder in the front yard, a paintbrush in her hand, her skirts tied in knots around her knees. She got one board on the roof of the porch painted the faintest shade of purple—most of the paint dotting her skin—then she stopped. Holding out her arm so she could see all the paint spots she'd made, she called down to Papa, "Say, Ivar."

Papa hummed back.

"I think I know a better thing to do with this paint."

"What's that?" Papa asked.

"Throw it," she said, quick as a whip, and splattered Papa with a big old glob of paint. I giggled and Mama sprinkled paint down into my hair. She was laughing wildlike. A happy bird in a tree, she was flicking paint everywhere.

Papa was happy, too—howling and shouting at her to get down, so he could show her what to do with that paint, but Mama just kept flinging. I knew what to do. I went straight inside and pumped out some clear, cool water from the sink, then ran upstairs to the guest room, knowing Mama was just below one of those windows. Running out onto the porch roof, I gave a heave-ho to the pitcher and sprayed Mama with water.

She screamed like a banshee. I was afraid she'd fall off the ladder, but no, she came scrambling up onto the roof after me. I had a head start, so I made it all the way through the house and out to the garden before she tackled me. In a frenzy of wiggling and laughing, she tickled me until I couldn't breathe, Papa doing the same to her, the two of us doing it back to him. We laughed until we cried, then we went on down to the creek with peach pit soap to wash out all the paint.

Papa and I laughed to remember that day. I wiggled on his chest in the waves of his laughter, then we were quiet. "We had fun, Papa. We were all good friends. Why weren't we enough to make Mama stay?"

He took a deep breath, then let it out in a whistle. "Maybe that's it. We're so busy looking for the reason your mama left, we can't be sad that she's gone."

I didn't answer him, mostly because I didn't know what to say, but I think part of the reason was that we couldn't believe she was gone. She'd packed up and walked out as if she was leaving a hotel. How could a mama, any mama, do such a thing? It wasn't supposed to happen. I tried to make myself think that it hadn't.

I just about had myself believing it was all a mix-up of some kind by Sunday morning. I was in the garden weeding the beds, telling myself Mama'd just gone off with one of her women's-group friends for the weekend and the note she'd left got blown away. It was almost working. The story was just about sticking in my mind, when Mary came charging through our back gate, shouting, "Is it true? Did your ma really leave?"

I felt like jabbing her in the foot with the hand shovel I held. Instead, I ignored her and swore to myself that I'd get back at her by telling everybody at school how she'd kissed Gary Journiette behind the church two Sundays before and told me his lips tasted like saltwater taffy.

Since I was quiet, she kept buzzing around me like some ear-hurting horsefly. "Is she really gone? You know what it means when a woman runs off like that?"

"What?"

"She's gone off with a man."

I wanted to tell her she was crazy, but Mary knows all about the things women and men do with each other. She's in the sixth grade like me, but she got held back a year, so she's already twelve. Plus, her sister April's nineteen and knows all about courting. Mary said she's waiting until she's twenty to even look a boy in the eye. She couldn't pass that promise by Gary Journiette, I bet.

Still, best friend and boy knowing aside, Mary had no right to be yacking away about my mama like that. I shook a clump of dirt at her. "You shut that mouth of yours before I plant something in it."

Mary dropped down to her knees, saying, "Oh Nissa, I didn't mean no harm. Lord forgive me. I'd rather ask the Pope if he peed. I'm sorry."

I giggled imagining the fat old Pope Mrs. Carroll had a picture of over her piano picking up all the skirts of his long white gown to take a pee.

"You aren't mad?" she asked.

"I sure am," I shouted. "You come around here spreading rumors about my mama like it was God's good news."

"I didn't mean it like that."

"What did you mean?"

"Don't fight with me, Nissa. Is your ma gone or not?"

It hit me like a punch in the heart. Mama was gone. I was crying before I could get my lips apart to say, "Yes."

Mary was hugging me as I cried. I got her shoulder all wet before she said, "Nissa, you cry anymore and these weeds are going to grow until they choke us."

We laughed, then Mary looked down at her dress. To hug me, she'd left the flagstone path and kneeled in the flower bed with me. Her nice pink dress was spotted with brown mud. "I'm heaven bound. Ma's going to kill me for this."

"Come on." I rushed her into the kitchen. Rubbing it with soap, I yanked her dress up to the sink and started pumping water.

Mary was teetering on her tiptoes shouting, "Don't you want me to step out of it?"

"Naw." I let go of the pump and started rubbing the fabric together like I'd seen my Grandma Dee do when she tried to get grass stains out of my overalls.

Mary watched me work. After a bit of rubbing, I stood up and rinsed the fabric. It looked a tad brown, but there was nothing a little ring through the washer wouldn't fix.

"Thanks."

"Sure thing," I said. "How about some lemonade?"

She nodded. We took our drinks out into the garden. After we were quiet for a bit, she said, "You know Nissa, if your ma doesn't come back, your pa's going to start looking for a new wife."

"Mama's coming back." I didn't believe it myself, but I

wasn't going to have Mary talking bad about my mama again.

"If she don't, he'll have to find a new wife like Old Man Carson did when his wife died. Someone's got to take care of you and the house and the garden and all."

I stared at Mary until my eyeballs crossed just like Mama taught me. "People don't get married so they can have maids!" I'd heard Mama say it a thousand times and I was glad to say it right. "If they do, then they might as well get a divorce."

"Is that why your ma left? She didn't want to be your pa's maid?"

"Mama wasn't anybody's maid. Besides, how am I supposed to know why she left? Did I follow Mama? Did she tell me where she was going? No! No! No!" I was shouting so loud I could hear my voice ringing in my ears.

"Sorry."

"You seem awful sorry today, Mary Carroll. Maybe you should go home before you do something else to hurt me."

"I didn't mean nothing."

"Then go and be nothing. I don't want to talk to you anymore." I took her glass and went into the house. As soon as I heard the back gate close, I regretted what I had said. Mary was a good friend. She just couldn't help but tell you everything that came into her head or she felt like she was lying, and lying was a sin.

Sometimes my friendship with Mary wore me out. Spending time with her was like a trip through a ringer washer. We'd start out laughing and hugging, then somebody'd say the wrong thing and we were ringing each other through. Times like those I thought it'd be just as easy to go on home and never see Mary again, but then I'd miss the grub hunting, the trips to Minkie's for saltwater taffy, the long talks about boys and bullfrogs. No, Mary and I were friends for life.

Things were about the same with Mama and me. Mama's mood shifted like a change in the weather. If her skies were clear, we'd be hand in hand racing down the bank of Sutton's Creek hunting up wildflowers to replant in the garden or carving boats out of used-up candle wax that Mama had pressed into a gravy boat for shape and watching them sail on the ripply waves. But when Miss Chessie Roubidoux started coming by to ask Mama to stop playing her music so loud or Clem Thibodeaux went on in church about the unholiness of women acting as men's equals, they'd push thunder and lightning into her day. Mama would turn wild and almost wicked. She'd strip off all the sheets on her bed and tie them into knots or break the rocks she dug out of the garden into tiny pieces. Then it was just good to stay out of her way.

One time, I made the mistake of asking her to go flower picking when she was in a foul mood and she turned on me, shouting, "Do I look like I give a tinker's dam about flowers?"

I could feel her anger inside me, squeezing. "No."

Mama closed her eyes and pressed her lips together. She rubbed my shoulders, saying, "I'm sorry, Nissa. I've got a rattler's temper. Your Grandma Dee used to say I'm made of rage and pixie dust. One minute, I'm as happy as a fairy, next I'm ready to chop everything down with an axe."

I was scared to think Mama might feel like raising an

axe to me. She sat down on the back steps and stared out at the garden. "It's best if we make a pact. When I'm in a no-account ugly mood, we stay clear of each other, and when I've got pixie dust to spare, you and I are off to the land of your choice." She turned to me, smiling.

"All right," I said, and I believed Mama could never do a violent thing to me.

She hugged me and everything was fine again. The storm was over and I had my mama back. I knew Mama shifted, so I tried to shift with her—know her mood and make my choices. If it was a bad day, Mary and I would go grub hunting.

It didn't seem like I had that choice anymore. Mama had just up and left. I wondered if it was because she was in a foul mood she couldn't shake. It didn't matter though, because mamas weren't supposed to leave. That was a sin, too.

I thought about looking in the Bible for what it said about the sin of mothers who leave their children. What if Mary—the mother of Jesus—up and walked out on Joseph and their baby? Bible mothers didn't do such things. I was no baby Jesus, but Mama shouldn't have walked out on me. I started pacing the hallway, telling myself, "She'll be back. She'll be back."

It didn't make me feel any better. I was no good at believing lies. Accepting the fact that Mama wasn't coming back, I started thinking about what Mary had said. Would Papa really start courting another woman? No sir. No how. Papa loved Mama. He told me so and Papa never lied.

Keeping Secrets

JUST BECAUSE PAPA AND I KNEW MAMA WAS GONE DIDN'T MEAN the whole town of Harper had to find out. Of course, if Miss Chessie Roubidoux got even a whiff of trouble from our place, she'd be making up stories and spreading them about faster than thistledown in a windstorm. One year, she had everyone in town believing Mama practiced voodoo on account of the fact that she drank hibiscus tea. Miss Chessie was walking past our place on her way to the post office and she saw me and Mama sitting out on the porch sipping our fresh, brewed-in-the-sun hibiscus tea. She stopped in the street and stared at us, the dust settling on her shiny shoes. Wiping the sweat from her face with the handkerchief she kept hanging over her belt, Miss Chessie said, "What on earth are you drinking, Heirah Rae Bergen?"

Mama held up her glass and shook it a little so the flower petals in the tea would float around a bit. I could tell by the smile on her face that Mama was thinking up a good answer. "Hibiscus tea."

I was disappointed. I usually got a good laugh over

watching Miss Chessie stomp off after Mama served her up a little just deserts.

"Hibiscus tea? What is that? Some voodoo brew you picked up from them colored folk down at the Crocked Gator?"

Mama was good friends with the folks down at the Crocked Gator Cafe. We were one of the only white families in there on any given day. I loved their alligator jambalaya. It was so hot, it made my mouth itch for days. Most white folks thought it was a sin to mix with black folks, but Mama didn't give a hoot. Neither did Papa. I didn't even bother thinking about it.

Now Miss Chessie, she thought all black folks were evil because she thought they were into voodoo magic. She was sure voodoo was devil worship. Mama just played right along with Miss Chessie's stupid beliefs.

"Why yes, Chessie. This is straight from a witch doctor's kitchen." Mama held her tea up higher. "It'll shrivel the kidneys of my enemies." Mama took a big gulp.

I bit my lip to keep from giggling as Miss Chessie glared at Mama's glass of tea. She said, "You're evil, Heirah Rae Bergen. And I'm going to see that this entire town knows it."

Mama licked her lips. "You do that, Chessie."

Miss Chessie stomped off shouting, "A woman like you shouldn't be allowed to have children." She turned back to say, "With your evil ways, you'll make that sweet girl just like you!"

Mama squeezed my hand, saying, "She'll be just like herself." She stood up, went to the porch railing, then raised up her glass so Miss Chessie could see it. "Here's to your health, Chessie!"

Miss Chessie just shook her head then charged into the post office all ready to spread lies about Mama. I was a bit afraid of what Miss Chessie might say, knowing how folks in Harper can be so mean to Mama, but Mama just sat back down and laughed.

"That woman's a lunatic," she said.

"What's that?"

"Well, she's not really a lunatic like the folks who are too crazy to know their day from their night, but Chessie Roubidoux has got some of the zaniest ideas I've ever heard. Hibiscus tea a voodoo brew." Mama shook her head a bit and laughed.

Our tea wasn't a magical potion, but folks didn't talk to Mama in church for close to a month after that. Some of the kids in school threw rocks at me if I tried to talk to them during recess and called me Witchy. Papa tried to put an end to it all by running an article about what voodoo really is next to a recipe for hibiscus tea. His plan didn't work though. His boss, Mr. Jonah Hess, would only run the tea recipe because he didn't want to be spreading no devil worship with an article on voodoo.

Harper's what Mama calls a canned town. Sometime, long ago, everyone in Harper canned their beliefs to preserve them. No one changes their mind in Harper. Things are as they've always been because the people are still thinking like they're living in 1857. Miss Chessie was the queen of the old thinkers, so she was always talking about how bad Mama was.

Over the weekend, no one even said a word about Mama being gone. I guess no one thought much of it because she went off on little jaunts to here and there once or twice a month. But if Miss Chessie started making up stories—there was no holding back all the kids at school. They'd be telling lies, calling names, and throwing rocks all over again.

To protect Mama and myself, I decided I'd tell the kids at school that Mama was off visiting her sister. They'd believe that for a month or two because I'd make them believe it. After a time, I'd have to come up with a new lie.

The Lord doesn't like lying, but as I saw it, I was keeping those kids from doing evil things. If they knew Mama was gone for good, they'd be sure to rub me raw inside with all their nasty ribbing. I was keeping them from sinning by telling a lie. I guess it was a little white sin to avoid a bunch of bigger sins.

I learned all about sins from Mary. Her family's Catholic. Her brother Teddy says that means their Bible's bigger, but Mary set me straight. She says it means they believe a man called the Pope, who lives way off in Europe somewhere, is the king of their religion. They've also got a different type of praying and a complicated system for identifying sins. You see, there's mortal sins and cardinal sins and a whole bunch of other kinds I don't remember. Anyway, mortal's the worst. It means doing something awful like killing somebody. If you do terrible things like that, then you've got to ask forgiveness for forever and become a monk or a nun. With the little sins you just say "God forgive me" and go on your way.

So, I got up Monday morning all ready to lie, then said, "Forgive me, God," and went off to breakfast.

Papa had made scrambled eggs and opened a jar of Grandma Dee's marmalade. He knew I loved eggs and marmalade. I said good morning and he said it back, but he kind of mumbled it like he was thinking of something else. Then I looked up and saw he was watching me. He watched me sit down and kept right on staring.

"Have I got my shoes on the wrong feet?" I stuck them out in front of me to take a look.

Papa laughed. "No, I just wondered how you're feeling this morning?"

I knew if I thought about it, I'd feel awful. There was a cold spot in my heart and even thinking about Mama made it grow bigger, so I said, "I'm doing all right."

Papa sat down next to me and leaned over the table to ask, "Is there anything you want to talk about?"

I could feel myself start to shake on the inside, so I blurted, "Can Mary and I walk to school together?"

Papa knew I'd walked to school with Mary since the first grade when she and her family moved to Harper from somewhere in Pennsylvania. He leaned back and sighed real big. "That's fine with me, Neesay."

I kept my eyes on the eggs so Papa wouldn't ask me any more questions, but I couldn't keep myself from hearing Mama's voice say, "Them eggs look like frog brains to me. I remember when Tracy Latner smashed a big old frog under his boot. When he picked his foot up, the brains were all over the ground looking just like scrambled eggs."

I dropped my fork. I could never eat my eggs if Mama

told that story. Even remembering it was enough to make my stomach tremble. "Papa, can I just have some toast?"

Papa stood up to make some. "Thinking of frogs were you?" he asked.

"Yeah," I whispered.

"Me, too," Papa said.

I couldn't hold Mama back any longer. She was on my mind and it was making my whole body sad. "Where do you think she is, Papa?"

He came to sit next to me real quick. "Wherever she is, Nissa, I know she's safe."

"How do you know?"

"The Lord would tell me if she was in trouble." Papa rubbed my hand as he told me that. He talked with the Lord all the time. Sometimes he even prayed out loud while he was driving so we'd have a safe journey to wherever we were going. If the Lord told Papa Mama was all right, well then, she was. For the Lord is the last one in the universe to lie.

I never ate the toast Papa made because Mary came for me just as it popped up. She tapped at the back door, saying, "You going to school today, Nissa?"

Papa looked at me and said, real quiet so Mary couldn't hear, "You don't have to go if you don't want to."

"I'm coming, Mary," I said, looking at Papa so he knew I was all right with going to school. There was no way I could spend the day in the house with all the things that reminded me of Mama inside it. I went to the back door.

Papa followed me with the toast in his hand. "Take the toast. You can eat it on your way to school."

"I'm not hungry, Papa." I opened the door.

"No hug?" Papa asked, as I closed the door behind me.

I smiled the best I could, then stepped back inside to give Papa a hug. It was like he swallowed me up for a second, warmed me to the bone just to say how much he loved me. And for an instant, I thought everything would be okay.

Then I was outside walking down Quince Road on my way to school with Mary beside me, swinging her lunch pail so it hit the fence alongside us. That old pail was full of dings from that fence. Her mama was always after her to stop, but Mary said the sound reminded her of the clanking of the tin cup that hung from their well in Pennsylvania. I was wishing I was Mary lying there in a Pennsylvania bed listening to a clanking cup. I wouldn't be missing my mama so.

"I'd just die if my ma left," Mary said, as we went past Old Man Benson's windmill.

"Don't talk about it."

"What are you going to tell everybody at school? You know how they like making up stories about your mama. Teddy even thinks she's a witch."

"Your brother's a blockhead." I marched a little ahead so Mary would leave me alone for a bit. But, she'd put Teddy into my head and I couldn't shake him out.

Teddy Carroll was a snot-faced brat. He tattled if Mary and I went to the Crocked Gator because Mary's mama said we couldn't. He dumped mud and sting weed into my boots when Mary and I went for a dip in the river. I'll be darned if he didn't find them no matter where I hid them. To set him square on my bad side forever, he was afraid of Mama. If he was on the front porch when Mama walked by the Carrolls',

Teddy would run scared into the house. He even hid behind Mrs. Carroll when he saw my mama in church and he was going on eight years old. What a pansy.

It was on account of Teddy's attitude toward Mama that the Carroll boys didn't walk to school with us anymore. When Mary and I first became friends, I walked with the whole Carroll clan to school—April, Simon, Mary, Teddy, and Little Anthony, when he was old enough. Now that April's doing the books for the Thibodeaux brothers at the feed store and Teddy and I aren't on speaking terms, it's just me and Mary, and sometimes I wish it was just me.

Mary grabbed my arm to make me stop when we were in sight of the school. She said, "You didn't say what you were going to tell everybody at school."

As I stared at the old gray building with the crooked front door, Mary added, "If I don't know, I can't help you keep your story up."

I was going to tell her to say Mama was at her sister's, but then I saw Peter Roubidoux standing on the playground with Teddy Carroll and Missy LaFavor pointing at me. Peter was Miss Chessie's nephew and if he had tales to tell, they came straight from his aunt who was forever reading people's mail and making up stories. As Mama always said, "The truth is damned with Chessie Roubidoux. She'd tell Jesus that Peter sold him out to the Romans."

If Peter knew about Mama, then everyone did and I wasn't going to hide behind any lies. "They know," I said, staring at Peter Roubidoux and hoping I could conjure up a hex to make his tongue fall out.

"Do you want to go back home?"

Part of me did. In fact, if my body had cooperated with my mind, I would have run home, but I was stiff. I just stood there and stared.

"Nissa?"

"I'm going to give Peter Roubidoux a shiner." I started walking, and no matter how much Mary fussed about fighting with a boy, I just kept right on going until I was a foot away from Peter.

"Didn't think you'd be coming, Nissa. With your Mama running off like she did, I figured——"

I didn't give Peter a chance to tell me what he figured. I punched him right in the left eye and knocked him flat on his butt. He hopped up, grabbing his eye and screaming like I'd plucked it out. Teddy was shouting and calling me a hussy. Mary boxed him in the ear, but he kept shouting.

Our teacher, Mrs. Owens, came running over waving her hands in the air, shouting, "Stop this fighting! Stop it! Stop it! Stop it!"

We all hushed up. She asked, "Who's involved here?" Outside, Mrs. Owens's vision was so bad, she couldn't count her own fingers. She squinted down at us to get a fix on who we were. Sometimes, if you kept real still, she thought you were someone else and you didn't get in trouble until she sorted out the truth. Peter usually pulled that trick, then stayed out of school the next day so she couldn't catch him in it, so I yelled, "It's Nissa Bergen and Peter Roubidoux and I punched him in the eye!"

"Why in Heaven's name would you do that, Nissa Bergen?"

"He was saying bad things about my mama."

"Does that give you the right to hit him?"

When I didn't answer, Mrs. Owens asked, "Would your mama do such a thing?"

There was a chorus from Peter, Missy, and Teddy. They all yelled, "She sure would!"

I was ready to pull up a tree, I was so mad. Mama wouldn't lay one hurting finger on a child, even one as ugly and mean as Peter Roubidoux. Then I felt guilty. Mama wouldn't want me hitting nobody. I was being twisted into knots and I just couldn't take it. I cut out of there and ran for the woods. Mary tried to follow me, but I heard her brother Simon calling her back. I wanted to run until I passed out, so all the crazy feelings inside me would leave me alone. Funny. Mama left me and all I wanted was to be alone.

Hiding Hiding

I WENT TO THE CREEK TO WATCH THE WATER FLOW OVER THE rocks. I loved how clean and shiny those rocks looked—like new souls, Mama used to say. I wished I could wash my soul until it glowed like that. Hitting Peter Roubidoux was a darn fool thing to do all around. God doesn't take kindly to acts of violence. Neither does my papa. He said anyone who had to fight with her hands didn't believe in the strength of her own soul. Besides which, my hand hurt. My knuckles were so swollen they looked like I'd pumped them full of air.

I stuck my hand in the cool water to make the swelling go down. I could have sat there forever, my hand turning numb, my mind drifting off to nothing as I watched the gnats play over the water. Then I heard rustling behind me. My first thought was that Peter Roubidoux had come for his revenge. I even had a rock gripped in my fist, just in case. But it was Mary. She'd left school to come find me. That would make her mama spitting mad, but it made me feel just a little bit happy.

"You all right, Nissa?" she asked, staying clear of me.

"I'm not going to hit you."

Mary came down to the creek, saying, "I know that."

"What'd Mrs. Owens say?" She always babbled on about the punishment she'd give to kids, even if they weren't there to hear her.

"That you'd have to apologize to the Roubidouxes and sit in the corner when you got back to school."

"I'm never going back to school," I said, throwing the rock I held at a nearby tree.

Mary said, "You can't stay out forever. How are you going to learn anything?"

"I'll get a tutor like Little Lord Fauntleroy."

"And where will you get the money for that? You'd have to find a million grubs just to pay the tutor to come meet you."

"Papa can teach me. He can even teach me Norwegian." I'd always wanted to learn Papa's language. He told me anything I wanted to know, like *fjord* means a real narrow gulf. Trouble was, I always forgot the words he told me.

"I wouldn't mind staying home with my pa. I never see him." Mary started tearing leaves off a bush and ripping them in half. Her papa worked a coal mine in Mississippi. He left before dawn and didn't come back till after dark. I was lucky to see my papa so much.

Speaking of papas always led to thinking of mamas, so I said, "You stay out of school and your mama will tan you purple."

"I'm already in trouble just coming out here."

"I didn't mean for you to get in trouble. I just wanted to be alone for a bit."

Mary threw the leaf bits in her hand out into the creek. They bobbed on the current, then disappeared under the water. Watching the leaves go under, Mary said, "I used to wish I had your ma. She always let you do what you wanted."

"She didn't let me jump off the roof." One time, I wanted to use my sheet as a parachute then jump into the garden and Mama assured me it wasn't a good plan.

"Of course not, but she'd let you stay up and look at the stars and climb trees and go frogging. My ma says I've got to act like a lady."

I looked at Mary who was squatted down like a catcher and laughed. "You aren't doing too good of a job."

"Shut your mouth, Nissa Bergen." She threw leaves at me. I pulled up some grass to throw back. We screamed and giggled, pulled and tossed until Mary slipped and fell into the creek. It's nothing but a knee-deep puddle down by the school, so she stood right back up. She splashed water at me. I can't swim worth diddly, but I can sling water better than a spitting catfish, so I shucked off my shoes and jumped in with her. I slapped the water. Mary screamed. We had ourselves a water fight. By the time we were done, we were soaked through and tuckered out. We went out to an open field to catch our breath and dry off in the sun.

Staring up at the clouds as they shuffled their way across the sky, I wondered what Mama was doing. Was she sitting outside a filling station drinking grape Nehi? Was she buying a train ticket to come home? Taking a bus to New Orleans? Wherever she was, I hoped she was missing me and Papa so much she'd come home soon.

"Do you think your ma will come back?"

"She can't stay away forever."

"Why not?"

"Because she loves me and you can't stay away from the things you love. It makes you grow old inside." I said this to myself as much as to Mary. I had to believe it or I'd disappear right there on the spot.

Mary and I were right about her mama. Mrs. Carroll took a belt to Mary for skipping school, then told her she couldn't do one thing with me for two weeks. Of course, Mary had to sneak over to my place to tell me this. I told her how sorry I was and she said it didn't matter much; she had her leather purse in her drawers during the spanking and we could always sneak around together. I just laughed. Mary never did listen to her mama and it was a good thing, too, or we'd never see each other.

Papa wasn't as mean as Mrs. Carroll. He never was, but he made me feel the weight of my sins. It wasn't anything he said, it was the sadness in his voice. It was heavy, like a sweater that's been left out in the rain. He sat on the back steps staring at the garden for the longest time. I didn't want to bother him, mostly because I knew what was coming, but partly because I hoped he was thinking of Mama and dreaming up a way to bring her home.

"Nissa." He said my name real low, like it was a dangerous secret.

I walked up to his back, but I hoped he wouldn't turn around. "Yes, Papa."

"What happened at school today?"

"I hit Peter Roubidoux for saying bad things about Mama."

"Why did you hit him, Nissa?"

"I, I . . ."

"Lost control?"

"Yes, Papa."

He patted the step beside him. "Sit down, Nissa."

I sat down, but I couldn't look at him. I knew he was ashamed of me.

He took a deep breath. "When you get upset you can yell and stomp all you want, Nissa, but you don't strike another person. You can't take that back."

"Yes, Papa."

"What are you going to do about this?"

I twisted my skirt around my finger. I wanted to think of something fit for the occasion, but I dreaded the fact that it would involve apologizing to Peter Roubidoux who no doubt would make me suffer. "I could make him some cookies and take them over to say how sorry I am."

"Are you?"

"Well, I'm sorry I hit him, but I still want him to pay for saying bad things about Mama."

Papa stood up. "He will, but not because of you, Nissa. His sins are between him and God."

Papa walked into the house and I wondered just how God kept track of all those sins—mortal or whatever. Did He try and remember them all? Was there a golden book of sins up in Heaven like Mary says? And when he made people pay for their sins, did he take a belt to them or talk it out like Papa did? I was voting on the long talks with God. I'd feel awful, but maybe I could get a few questions in—like why do babies die? Where do dogs go when they pass on? Did He make hurricanes or was that the devil's doing?

It didn't matter anyway. Peter Roubidoux probably wouldn't listen even if God was teaching the lesson. He was sleeping half the time in school and Teddy told Mary he put cotton in his ears when his mama scolded him. I'd seen him do it for revivals, too.

"Be the better person," that's what Papa told me, so I made him a batch of snickerdoodles. I was tempted to use a tablespoon instead of two teaspoons of cream of tartar to make Peter's mouth sting, but that wouldn't be a fitting thing for a better person to do. I even added a little extra sugar on top to make them real sweet.

Peter's papa was on the front porch when I got there. He was rocking in the chair by the door, his felt hat pulled down over his eyes, and his stocking feet up on the railing. Eliah Roubidoux was close to seven feet tall. Everyone called him the Harper Giant, but he always swore that he had three brothers in Georgia who were taller than he was.

I stood on the steps with my plate of cookies, hoping he'd notice me. He didn't move. "Mr. Roubidoux," I said, real quiet, in case he was sleeping.

He pushed his hat back, saying, "I saw you, girl. I was just taking a look to see what kind of girl could turn my boy's eye blacker than night."

"I'm sorry, sir."

"Sorry?" He sat up straight. I was afraid he was going to

stand up and then I would have to hightail it out of there. He was way too scary to face when he was mad and at his full height. It was like facing Goliath without a slingshot. He stayed in his seat, though, and said, "My boy Marshall said Peter was trash talking your mama."

"Yes, sir."

"Then he deserved a sock in the eye. Boys aren't to disrespect their elders."

"Yes, sir."

"I was just a mite disappointed that the first fight my boy lost was to a girl, but I don't suppose I was all that surprised seeing as how you're Miss Heirah's girl."

I wanted to ask just what exactly he meant by that, but I held up the cookies instead. "I came to apologize and give Peter these."

"Apologize my aunt's bunions! You give me those cookies and you hold your head high, girl. You put that disrespectful chit in his place."

He took the plate. His hands were probably big enough to cover it from side to side. "Now get out of here before my boys see you."

"Yes, sir." I stepped off the porch and started home. I wasn't sure just how I was supposed to feel about all that. Should I be mad at Mr. Roubidoux for saying my mama taught me to fight, if that's what he meant? Then again, I didn't apologize like I told Papa I would. Who was the better person in the end? Me? Peter? Or Mr. Roubidoux? Papa, I guess. He had the best idea of us all. Don't hit nobody.

I never told Papa what happened, but he said I would

have to go back in a week or so for the plate. I shivered with the idea of meeting up with Peter Roubidoux on his home ground. Then there was school. I asked Papa about it at supper that night. We had cold chicken left over from the church picnic.

"Do I have to go back to school, Papa?"

"You can't hide from your mistakes, Nissa."

It wasn't my mistakes I was worried about. By that time everyone probably knew Mama had left and I just didn't want to hear what the kids had to say about it. "But they're all talking about Mama."

Papa didn't talk for a minute, then he just started saying things. "I wonder if Heirah thought of such things when she walked out? This town is going to be bursting with stories. No one's going to give either of us a moment's peace."

I felt myself twisting up inside. I was mad at Mama for leaving. Mad at Papa for talking her down and angry at myself for caring what other people thought. "You're mad at Mama because you don't want people to talk about us?"

Papa shook his head. "I'm sorry, Nissa. I shouldn't have said that. I just, well, your mama does things without thinking sometimes and it hurts us more than it hurts her. You know what I mean?"

I did. When Mama saw that Mrs. Owens had given me a lesson book for kindergartners when I was in the second grade, she took me straight to school and told Mrs. Owens she should turn the school over to a person who could at least see the lessons she was teaching. Mrs. Owens started to cry. Mama said, "If the truth brings tears, then you better change it."

I wanted to do something to make Mrs. Owens feel better. She didn't see well, but there's nobody in Harper who knows more about history and math than her. She can do long division in her head and recite every speech Jefferson Davis ever made.

Mama dragged me out of the school and swore she wouldn't send me back, but Papa convinced her it was an honest mistake. Mama never apologized and Mrs. Owens didn't so much as look at me for weeks.

Mama did what she wanted to when she wanted to do it. It didn't matter who was in her way or what happened afterward. She just did it. Grandma Dee said Mama slipped into her own little world sometimes where Mama was the only resident. I wished I could go to that world. Get out of Harper, Louisiana, and go with Mama.

"Nissa?" Papa looked at me like I'd been sprouting flowers out of my ears. "Where'd you go?"

I'd drifted off into my thoughts. I guess I was a lot like my mama. "Sorry, Papa. I was just thinking."

"About?"

"Nothing much."

"We were talking about school."

"I don't want to go. Like you said, I won't get a moment's peace."

"We aren't going to hide, Nissa. You go back to school tomorrow and ignore those kids. You know your mama loves you and that's what counts." He kissed me on the top of the head and took his lemonade out into the garden.

Did she love me? Do you leave the people you love? God, I hope so. Or do I? I was getting dizzy with all the thoughts swirling around in my head. I went upstairs for a nap to let everything quiet down for a bit.

Weathering the Storm

I DREAMED OF ROSE PETALS IN THE MOONLIGHT. MAMA'S ROSES looked black at night. Mama said they soaked up the moonlight so you could taste it in their petals and feel as calm and cool as the moon. I woke up with the moist feeling of a rose petal on my tongue.

It was dark out. Papa had opened my windows to let the cool air in and I could hear someone down in the garden. Mama walked in the garden when she was upset. A garden's never silent, even at night. There are bugs chirping and munching, breezes blowing petals, and mice, coons, and owls hunting up their meals. Mama loved to just walk and listen. She said, "I forget my troubles and just wonder what kind of bug goes whaaa-whurrr-whaaa-whurrr."

I prayed it was Mama in the garden. I could almost see her as I got up—the long skirt of her white nightgown swaying over the flagstones. But when I went to the window, I saw Papa down there. He was still in his day clothes as he cut away dead leaves. He was keeping Mama's garden just as she liked it. He was probably hoping she'd be coming back to see it. I wished he was right.

Sitting there, seeing Papa bent down in Mama's flowers, I figured I needed my own flowers, something to keep me calm. The next morning, I got up before Papa. I left a note to say I'd gone to skip rocks before school. I went to the wading pool and picked out the best, shiniest stones I could find, but I didn't skip them, I just tucked them in my pocket. I went out to the open field to lay down and watch the clouds drift over me, but I fell asleep. Mary found me there.

"Get up, girl! We'll be late for school and I'll be killed for sure."

Jumping to my feet, I said, "Won't Teddy tattle if he sees us together?"

"Not if Simon has anything to say about it. He told Pa Teddy was ribbing you right along with Peter. Papa gave him the belt."

I wasn't glad Teddy got a whipping, but I hoped it would keep his mouth shut. Walking up to the school, I could see everybody staring at me like I was a bear sauntering in from the woods. They probably thought I'd tear into anybody who'd say a word about my mama. I hoped they did, then maybe they'd keep quiet.

Mrs. Owens had me sit in the corner all morning and Peter made faces at me thinking Mrs. Owens couldn't see him, but she saw with more than her eyes. "You make one more monkey face, Mr. Peter Roubidoux, and you'll be joining Miss Bergen."

"Yes, ma'am."

I did my math there in the corner. When I heard kids whispering and started thinking they were talking about Mama, I just put my hand in my pocket and rubbed my stones. Thinking of how their smooth surface is like the darkness of night when everything's calm and there for the listening to, I forgot all about those snits and divided 342 by 12, then 571 by 7. The morning passed and I was thinking I might really live through the day.

At recess, Missy LaFavor ruined everything. Mary and I were playing jacks on the big stone behind the school and Missy came up with her hair filled with silly ribbons. She shouted, "My mama says yours is going to jail."

I wasn't even going to answer her. It was stupid to think Mama would get arrested for anything. But, Missy kept going. "Mama says you get put in prison for abandoning your kids."

Abandoning. It was a word that made me think of a crying baby all alone in an empty old house with broken windows and slivery wooden floors. Mama didn't abandon me. She'd left me, but I wasn't alone. I had Papa. I wanted to make Missy LaFavor swallow jacks, but I said, "My mama's gone to New Orleans to learn to dance." It'd always been a dream of Mama's so I could have been telling the truth. She might have gone to the dance school she always talked about—Marie Fontaine's on La Rue de la Rouge in New Orleans.

"That's a lie and you know it!" Missy shouted.

Peter Roubidoux added, from several feet away, "Everybody knows your mama ran off. I wonder who she's with?"

Mary jumped up, yelling, "You shut your mouth, Peter Roubidoux! Or I'll stretch your lip over your head and sew it there!"

I just shoved my hand in my pocket and pictured myself

floating on a cloud beneath the stars. Those kids didn't know a thing about my mama. They were just talking to hear themselves say mean things. Maybe it made them feel big and important like Peter's Aunt Chessie. Everyone thought she was such a fine lady—keeping a moral eye on the people of Harper. I wanted to give them all the evil eye.

Mrs. Owens came and sent Missy and Peter to the back corners of our classroom, but it was hopeless. Everybody at school was whispering about Mama running off. My head was filling up with their ugly rumors. I was sure it was going to burst, so I ran straight back to Main Street when Mrs. Owens rang the final bell. Running jogs up my thoughts until they just fall to pieces.

I was standing in the post office, catching my breath, when I heard old Miss Chessie talking to Mrs. Linzy about Mama. Mrs. Linzy was getting her mail and I was fetching ours. Mrs. Linzy's box is behind the counter on account of the fact that she's the preacher's wife and gets lots of mail. Ours is at my eye level in the entry hall, so I was behind the big support post with the wanted posters on it. Ducking below mug shots of Myron Journiette, the king of white lightning, and his tax-evading cousin Jesse, I could listen without being seen.

I heard Miss Chessie say, "Did you hear about Heirah Rae?"

Mrs. Linzy whispered, "What now?"

"She walked out on Ivar with another man." Miss Chessie sounded as if she were reading the address off an envelope, like talking trash about my mama was part of her regular duties.

I knew just what she meant, too. I'd found out about adultery in my religion class at school. We were studying the Ten Commandments. There's a Commandment about adultery. Actually, our Bible says, "Thou shalt not covet thy neighbor's wife."

I hadn't understood the coveting part; then our teacher, Mrs. Owens, had said coveting meant stealing. I wanted to know if she was saying men just walked right into other men's homes and snatched their wives. I raised my hand real high and waved it around. Mary saw me waving my arm and pulled it down, whispering, "What are you doing that for? The bat can't see you."

"What's she mean by stealing another man's wife?"

"Baby making," Mary giggled. "Adultery means going off with someone you aren't married to and baby making."

I didn't want anyone saying bad things about my mama. She may have left, but she wasn't doing anything bad. I was ready to march right out from behind that post and tell those women they had their skinny noses in the wrong laundry. Then Mrs. Linzy up and said, "Ivar must be a wreck."

Miss Chessie snickered. She and Mrs. Linzy were just making fun of our family with their mean old gossip. I was so mad, I ran home without the mail.

The house was empty in an airy kind of way. The windows were open and the curtains were blowing frantically as if the outside were rushing into the house. I wanted to scream and bring Mama and Papa running, but nobody was there. I just wandered around and let my thoughts drift with the wind.

* * *

I kept smelling sawdust. I couldn't figure out what'd make me think of that bitter old dust, then I remembered how, about a month back, Mama started smelling of it. Every Saturday after Papa left for the store, Mama would get dressed in her pink frock. She'd stopped wearing it on Sundays. Mama would leave saying she'd be going to tea with the ladies in her women's club. They're the ones who made signs saying things like "Give your Mom the Vote," or "Women can run your home, why not your state?" Years ago, they carried these signs during election times, trying to change people's ideas about women voting. Nowadays they write letters to senators and other people to put their votes to good use by asking for better treatment of women.

Mama said working together as a group is the only way women can make changes, but somehow I suspected she wasn't going to her women's group during March and April. I think she was really meeting the Sawdust Man. When Mama came home, her cheeks were darker than her dress and she always smelled like sawdust.

I'd never thought it was a man who'd made Mama red and stinky until Miss Chessie put the idea into my head with all her gossip. Damn that Chessie Roubidoux and damn that Sawdust Man. When Grandpa Jared finds a rat's nest, he douses it with gas and sets it on fire. That's what I would do to the Sawdust Man if I ever caught up to him, but I had no idea where he'd taken my mama.

No matter where Mama really was, the town of Harper was convinced she'd run off with another man. And I believed them. Why else would she sneak off without me and come back smelling of sawdust? For what other reason would she run off? The real question was, did she love her Sawdust Man more than me?

I started pulling the weeds in the hibiscus bed and got lost in that question for hours. I didn't come out the other side until I'd weeded the entire thing. I remembered the day in kindergarten when Mama came to get me from school because there was a storm brewing. The dark clouds rumbled over us as we walked and there was lightning stabbing at the ground on the horizon. The wind was whipping our clothes and tossing our hair as we stuck close together and pushed our way down Quince Road. Most of the other kids ran home. Those who lived farther out stayed on at school because it was safer than trying to make it to their houses.

I could barely hear Mama in all the noise, but she was singing "Lord Lead Us Home." I tried to remember the words so I could sing them too, but I got lost trying to hear just what Mama was singing. We made it to the front porch just seconds after the rain started coming down. Papa was upstairs pulling all the shutters closed. Mama pulled me inside and shut the door. Squeezing me tight, she said, "I'd just die if I didn't have my Nissa to love."

Mama loved me. That hadn't changed. Papa said it was her love for him that had shifted. I didn't understand how that could happen, but Mama always said, "A love between a man and a woman is like a kite. It's beautiful, and it drifts with the wind, but it's still tethered to the ground with a string and if that string breaks, there isn't anybody but God who can bring it back." The Sawdust Man had cut the string on Mama's love for Papa. I hated him. Whoever he was.

The Crocked Gator Cafe

EVERYBODY IN TOWN HAD AN IDEA OF WHO THE SAWDUST MAN was. Or so I thought by the way they looked at me when I walked down the street and just shook their heads like they were saying, "Poor child, her mama ran off with a barber" or "Her mama took up with a Texas oil rigger." I heard the rumors. Usually through April who heard everything at the feed store. Sometimes, I heard them firsthand—like in church. It was double sad to hear it there. People were talking Mama down and doing it in the Lord's house. Sinful, indeed. God's ears must have been burning.

The week after school let out, I was standing beside Papa in the church fellowship hall. People came up to shake his hand and ask after the news. I wasn't so dumb as to think the smiling ladies who held up their hands like they expected Papa to kiss them didn't know every little thing Papa wrote in the paper. They were always talking about this or that.

I'd had enough of their petty flirting, so I went over to the table with all the pictures Mr. Luc Journiette had taken at our church picnic, hoping I'd find one of Mama. I was searching a picture of a bunch of ladies setting out their baked goods when I heard Chessie Roubidoux and Lila Cardon chewing up Mama with their nasty gossip. Miss Roubidoux was sure bent on turning everybody in town against Mama. She up and said, "I'm shock sure I know who Heirah Bergen ran off with."

"Who?" Miss Cardon gasped.

Miss Roubidoux said, "Before she left, I saw her here and there with Ira Simmons and I haven't seen him since she left."

"Ira Simmons?" Mrs. Cardon sounded like she'd just heard Mama'd been kissing a dog or something.

Everybody knew Ira Simmons. He was the black man from up Biloxi way. He had family here in Harper and had come down to set up a shop for making furniture. He made the table in our kitchen and the desk in Papa's study without a single nail. I really liked Mr. Simmons. He had a habit of carrying little wooden balls in his pocket. When he got to talking, he'd roll them around in his hands. The scrape and churn of the balls gave a nice edge to his voice. He was a good man who was sweet on Rinnie Lee Sinclair, the lady who runs the Crocked Gator Cafe.

I was sick of hearing Miss Roubidoux spreading smelly old lies. I was about to start chucking pictures across the room and shouting, "Miss Chessie Roubidoux drinks whiskey!" She doesn't as far as I know, but I wanted people to realize what a fire-breathing beast she was. It was Mrs. Villeneuve who kept me from flying into a rage. She put her long black fingers over my shoulder and gave it a little squeeze.

I'm sweet on Mrs. Villeneuve. She's got the prettiest

hands in all of Harper. She can put her pinkie on a C and her thumb on the C an octave down—they're the longest fingers in the world, I'm sure. I just love to watch her play the piano. I don't get much chance, though. They only let her play when our pianist, Mrs. Geron, is ill.

Mrs. Villeneuve gave me a little shake, saying, "Don't you listen to those fools, child. They're talking lies."

Mrs. Villeneuve should know. Mr. Simmons rented her back room. I nodded to her. She smiled, then went upstairs where the black folks had to sit. We were the only Protestant church in town and nearly half the church was empty every Sunday, but the white folks didn't want to sit in the same room with the black folks. Mama used to say she'd like to poke people's eyes out so they couldn't see black nor white, then everybody could get along. Not with Chessie Roubidouxes in the world, I thought.

Miss Chessie was always talking bad about my mama and I had to find a way to set people straight, so I snuck out of there with a sorry to the Lord and ran to Mary Carroll's. She'd know what I should do.

Mary was counting her giving-money on the front porch when I got there. Her family goes to the church on the hill behind the post office.

"Mary," I gasped, flopping myself down on her steps.

"What are you running from?" Mary asked, squinting up at me. She's got little holes in her face from when she had the chicken pox and I always think they must hurt when she squints.

"Chessie Roubidoux said Mama ran off with Ira Simmons."

Mary dropped her giving-money and came to sit by me. At least she didn't say I told you so. I think that's why we're friends. She's as honest as my mama and most times she's as kind and thoughtful as my papa. "Well, that's a fool thing to say. Mr. Simmons was fixing the carts at the mine where Papa works three weeks ago. He doesn't have a truck or anything, so he stayed on there. Papa played cards with him at lunchtime. Papa said he's working for the railroad now—fixing boxcars or something."

"I didn't think it was true, Mary! I just wanted to stop the talk."

"Stop it? Are you ill? There's nothing that can keep Chessie Roubidoux from flapping her chicken lips."

"How about Miss Rinnie Lee? She's courting with Mr. Simmons, isn't she?"

"For as long as I can remember, but that isn't going to help. Miss Roubidoux isn't going to take Miss Rinnie Lee's word. You know that."

"Well, maybe she can get Mr. Simmons to come home."

"Not likely."

"I've got to try. Come with me."

"And miss church? Don't you want me to grow up?" Mary looked over her shoulder to see if her mama had noticed us.

"After then, meet me on the tracks."

"Sure thing."

"Mary?" Mrs. Carroll called from inside the house.

"Coming, Ma." Mary answered real calmlike as she waved frantically with her hand to get me to leave before anybody saw me. I jogged around the corner and saw Little

Anthony was in the backyard throwing rocks at the bird-bath. Seeing me, he started to come over to the fence, but I held a finger to my lips to let him know my presence was a secret. He held his finger up to say he'd keep it. I ran off.

The railroad tracks run by the feed store, then bore their way through the woods to the swampland west of town. On account of the boggy ground most everything on that side of Harper was on stilts to keep the places from sinking. The black folks lived in that part of town and I was afraid of it. Not because I thought there was any evil down that way, I just knew it had a magic all its own that I didn't understand.

Take voodoo, for instance. Mama told me that it's a religion like any other, but dead animals and spells are involved in there somehow. Mama just laughed at me when I talked about conjure. She said, "Just what's the difference between a conjure and a prayer, Nissa? They pray their way, we pray ours."

I said, "Does that mean there's voodoo gods in Heaven?"

Mama laughed, but I didn't think it was all that funny. The Bible says there will be no god before the one true God, so where did the voodoo gods fit in? Were they like the dukes to the king of England? I had no idea. I just knew I didn't like it when I saw little packets of spices hanging in a doorway. I knew then that there was voodoo magic in the house. Mama said they were to keep evil spirits out. Well, I didn't want to go inside, just in case they didn't work.

Voodoo was only part of the magic around Creechton Swamp. The people there had a magic all their own, one I couldn't quite catch on to. I'd see them on the back porch of the Crocked Gator dancing to the Creole music from the saloon down the street and I'd be under their spell. That music is so alive—it's like it's dancing with itself. The people are so happy and loud, I can feel them from the tracks up the hill. They move to the beat like they're part of it. If the band played loud enough, I'm sure the dancers could drift up in the air with it and fly away.

Mama can enter music like that—just take a ride with it—but I can't. I'd love to, but my body's just too darn clumsy. I'm stuck with watching.

I sat on the rail behind the Crocked Gator and watched. Miss Rinnie Lee's cafe's called the Crocked Gator because it's but a stone's throw from the swamp. And rumor has it the gators wade right up to the back porch because it's an honor to be in a crock of Miss Rinnie Lee's jambalaya.

No one was around that early on a Sunday morning because most folks were in church—whatever church they attended. Harper didn't have six hundred people in it, but we had seven churches. So, I sat there and stared at the back porch, watching the red-and-white checkered tablecloths blowing in the wind like they were listening to a tune I couldn't hear.

Mary finally showed up when Miss Rinnie Lee came out onto the porch with a laundry basket. "What have you been doing all this time?" Mary asked, running up to me all red faced and out of breath.

"Watching."

"I swear, Nissa Bergen, you are one strange girl."

54 The Year of the Sawdust Man

"Why do you say that?"

"You've been sitting here for two hours watching a back porch and you're asking me why I think you're strange?"

"Shush," I said, standing. "Come with me to talk to Miss Rinnie Lee."

"I'll come, but I'm not talking to anybody."

"You scared?"

"I don't know any of the folks down there. What am I going to say?"

"Fine." I marched down the hill. Miss Rinnie Lee was shaking out the tablecloths and putting them in a laundry basket.

"Can we help?" I asked.

Miss Rinnie Lee gave a little shout. "You frightened me, girl. Can't you and your mama use the front door like everybody else?"

"Sorry."

She laughed. "I was just teasing. Who's this?"

I stepped back to present Mary. "Mary Carroll."

"Jake Carroll's girl?" Mary nodded and Miss Rinnie Lee said, "Why your daddy was right nice to my Ira. He helped him up in that coal mine they had him working in."

"Yes, ma'am."

"Tell your daddy I'm much obliged. Mississippi's no place for a talented black man to show his stuff."

I'd read in Papa's paper about people in Mississippi dressed up in sheets, calling themselves the Ku Klux Klan, and burning black people's houses. I'd heard of black folks who'd been beaten for looking the wrong way at white folks or taking a white person's job or just acting uppity—

whatever that means. Louisiana wasn't any different. I hated it. I didn't see why God made people different colors in the first place. Shoot, if it wasn't the color of someone's skin that turned people mean—there'd be something else. Look at my mama. Most folks in Harper thought she was evil and what did she do? Drink hibiscus tea? Some sin.

"What brings you two here on a Sunday?" Miss Rinnie Lee asked.

I tried to ask her about Ira coming home, but it felt wrong. I would be asking about her private business. I had no right to do that, so I said, "I was just going to say how much I missed seeing Mr. Simmons around."

"Me, too," she laughed. "I miss your mama as well." She frowned. "I'm sorry she's gone, Miss Nissa."

"She'll be back." I said it as a reflex.

Miss Rinnie Lee turned away. She knew it wasn't true, just like I did. "Well, I know Ira misses her something awful. They were good friends."

Good friends? Women weren't friends with men. Especially not black men. I don't think there's anything wrong with it, but it just isn't done.

"Really?" I asked, wondering why Mama never told me she was friends with Ira Simmons.

"Sure," she nodded. Mary just stood there gawking at us like we were in our Skivvies or something. Miss Rinnie Lee said, "They were always talking over a cup of coffee or walking the tracks looking for wildflowers. They're a peculiar pair. A man who likes flowers and a white woman who likes colored folks."

Peculiar. That was it. Mama had found a man as

peculiar as she was. They *had* run off together. I nodded and tried to smile, but I was ready to cry. "Thank you, Miss Rinnie Lee. You have a good day now."

"You, too."

I ran up the hill. Mary caught up to me shouting "What's the matter? You heard her, they were just friends."

"Friends?" I turned to face Mary. "How many women do you know who are friends with a man?"

"I don't know."

"It doesn't happen, Mary. They ran off together."

"You don't know that. You don't even know why your ma ran off."

"Do you?"

"How could I?"

That was true. How could anybody but Mama know why she'd left or where she'd gone? I was shooting into the wind with all my guessing. If I wasn't careful, I'd hit something I didn't mean to, like me. I decided then and there not to think another wondering thought about Mama until she came back to tell me the truth.

Miss Lara Ross

I'D SEEN PAPA TRACE THE VEINS ON MAMA'S HAND AS THEY SAT and talked on the front porch. I knew he kissed her every morning before she went out to work in the garden, but she wasn't there anymore. Papa and I kept up Mama's garden, which made me believe he still loved Mama, but by that fall, I had my doubts.

In early October, he helped Miss Lara Ross out of her car. Everyone knows a lady can get out of a car by herself. For weeks I'd seen her step out, all long legs and smiles, before she walked into Mr. Minkie's store. She came back out a few minutes later with a small brown package no bigger than my clenched fist. She did it Saturday after Saturday, hoping Papa might get the hint. I was hoping she'd find worms in her sack. She had no right to be buzzing around my papa. Women like Miss Lara Ross did those flirty kinds of things. If you're unmarried at twenty-seven, as she was, you were watched for flaws and eager to hitch up before you dried up inside and couldn't make any babies.

She was lousy at flirting. Papa helped her out of her car

at church, then she walked right in without him. I hated her for taking Papa's hand with her soot-gray glove, then I hated her for passing my papa by like he was a hired driver once he'd helped her out. What upset me the most was the way Papa followed her up those steps with his eyes. He squinted as she reached the church door, then put his fedora on. At least he didn't smile.

Still, there was a real good chance Papa was thinking about courting her. I was stewing on Papa when we went into church. How could he be courting another woman? He was married. 'Sides which, it was a week away from his wedding anniversary. What kind of man would be looking at another woman so close to his anniversary? I prayed long and hard that God would turn Papa's head and heart back to Mama.

To get a little help, I ran straight to Mary's window after church. I tapped three times and she opened it up. Before she had a chance to speak, I blurted out, "Papa just helped Miss Lara Ross out of her car!"

"Really?" She thought a minute, then said, "Come on in."

I climbed through the window, then took a seat on April's bed. Mary sat across from me and asked, "How long has your ma been gone?"

"Almost five months." I whispered because I didn't want to believe it.

"She's never been away that long without calling." Mary started to tap her left foot. That's her thinking foot. "What did your pa say while he was helping Miss Ross?"

"Good morning, Miss Ross."

"Was he smiling?"

"No."

"Good." Mary nodded. "That means he's only being gentlemanly. He doesn't like her."

"You sure?"

"Have I ever lied to you?" Mary asked.

I knew she never really had, but it was a good time to tease her. I stood up to say, "You told me babies came with storks."

She giggled. "That's what my ma told me." We laughed together knowing Mrs. Carroll still thought we believed in Santa Claus, the Tooth Fairy, and the Baby Stork.

Mrs. Carroll liked me about as much as my papa liked Mary, which wasn't a lot. Anytime we got in trouble together, Mrs. Carroll blamed me and Papa blamed Mary. Which is okay I guess, considering Mary and I blamed each other.

"Mary Louise?" Mrs. Carroll called from the kitchen. "Who are you talking to?"

"Just Nissa, Ma!" Mary yelled back to her mother.

Mrs. Carroll showed up in the doorway, wiping her hands on a towel. "Do you ever use the door to come in this house, Nissa?"

"Yes, ma'am," I nodded, but to tell the truth, I can't remember the last time I did. Going through the door meant running the risk of meeting up with Mrs. Carroll or, even worse, Teddy.

"Well, I'd like to see you use it more often," Mrs. Carroll said.

"Yes, ma'am."

"Good." Mrs. Carroll left.

When I was sure Mrs. Carroll couldn't hear us, I said, "You sure Papa isn't sweet on Miss Ross?"

"Would you be?" Mary squinted. "She's got hairs poking out of her nose."

"I don't know what men like."

"No man likes hairs hanging out of a woman's nose."

I felt I could trust Mary's ideas on courting. They came straight from April, who had the Harper record for the most marriage proposals—a total of seven before she turned nineteen. She even showed me the ring Fenton Journiette gave her when she was eighteen. It was a diamond the size of a bread crumb on a silver band, but she was real proud of it. She held it up to the bare light bulb of her bedside lamp to make it shine.

"Are you going to marry him, April?" Mary had asked from her position on the floor next to April's bed.

April held the ring up to admire it. "Golly no."

"Why not?" I asked, squinting my eyes against the lamplight.

"If there's one thing I've learned after five years of dating and watching girls my age get married—you don't say yes to any man unless he has a piece of land to call his own."

"Or you end up pregnant and poor," Mary shouted. She'd heard April say it before. Mary always remembered everything April told her, so she knew an awful lot about men.

Still, I had to know from Papa himself. I sat on the front porch to wait for him to come home. Mr. Ira Simmons walked by as I sat there. Tipping his hat to me as he went by, I noticed him looking up at Mama's window. He'd been back in town for a week, but he didn't even do Mama the courtesy of killing all the talk about him and Mama by asking Miss Rinnie Lee to marry him. Sure enough, he and Miss Rinnie Lee were seen all around town together, but that didn't stop Miss Chessie. She kept right on flapping her lips, especially when Mr. Simmons went off on long trips for the railroad and such.

What I couldn't figure out was why he was walking past our place. Thinking on it for a minute, I realized Mr. Simmons didn't live anywhere near us. He lived down on Gambola Street right before Creechton Swamp. What was he doing walking by our house? He went to church over at the Holy Mountain where the black folks sing and dance every Sunday. Now that'd be celebrating the Lord, I thought, but Papa said dancing wasn't proper in a church. Dancing aside, I had to know what Mr. Simmons was doing going past our place on a Sunday morning.

I stood up and watched him turn down the hill toward the swamp, thinking how nice he looked in the gray trousers. He usually wore denims with the cuffs all folded up. I always saw him with a load of sawdust swishing around down there. Sawdust! Could he be the Sawdust Man? My heart was flip-flopping. Did he know where Mama was? If he did, why would he look at her window?

My life was turning into an endless pit of questions. Where was Mama? Why was Papa doing sweet things for Miss Lara Ross? What was Mr. Simmons looking for? My head was beginning to hurt. It was probably the heat, but I sure was glad when I saw Papa pull up in our old car. He'd have some answers.

As he walked up to the house with a frown on his face, I began to wish he'd taken a little longer coming home. He drives to church so we can take Mrs. Mabel. She lives down the street from us and I swear she's old enough to personally remember the color of Moses' eyes and it'd take her three years to walk to church, so Papa gives her a ride. And sometimes he stays for lemonade. Today would've been a good day for that. He looked mad enough to skin me, so he needed a little cooling off.

"Where've you been?" Papa asked, as he stepped onto the porch. He didn't like it if I ran off without telling him where I was going and I'd done a lot of that lately.

Suddenly, I felt kind of ashamed for doubting him. "Nowhere," I said.

Papa gave me a puffy-faced smile like a circus clown. He never was good at staying mad. He said, "Now how'd you get there? I hear tell they have great peaches in Nowhere, so I've been meaning to go myself."

Laughing, I said, "Papa."

"A lie for a lie," he said, opening the door. Then, quick as a wing beat, he tapped my nose. "Just to be fair."

"I was at Mary Carroll's," I said, following him into the house.

He was undoing his tie as he walked toward the kitchen. "What wonderful new mysteries did she uncover today? Did she explain how that big red spot got on the south side of the Mayor's house?"

"No." I sat down at the kitchen table. Everyone knew the mayor's wife put that spot on their house when she found out he was seeing a black woman. She said it was just a little reminder that he wasn't to sneak out on her with another woman ever again. I wondered what Mama would do if she found out Papa might be courting another woman. She'd probably paint Papa red so no woman would go near him.

"Then why'd you run to her house?"

Papa had probably seen me leaving church. He wasn't like Mama. He didn't come at you with the things you did. When I broke Mama's crystal angel, then tried to hide the broken parts in the poppy bed, she dug up the pieces and put them in a box. Shaking it in my face, so it rattled the glass and my nerves, she said, "What's this, Little Miss Hideabout?"

I confessed on the spot and dusted Mama's room for a month to pay for the angel. If I did something wrong and tried to hide it, Mama was on me like a mama bear on a hunter preying on her cubs—all claws and snarls. When she was mad at me, I felt it in the pit of my soul.

Not Papa. He didn't scare me. He just made me nervous. He'd talk me into a confession. I'd be telling him my deepest secrets before I even knew he was asking to hear them. It was like he was leading me to realize what I was doing and thinking, so I'd figure out when I'd done something wrong or needed to tell him the truth. He was so kind about it, I felt I had to tell him everything, but the best part was—I actually felt better when we were through talking even if I'd spilled grape juice on his only photograph of Grandma Nissa and Grandpa Knut.

I said, "I saw you helping Miss Ross out of her car today."

"And?" Papa was as slow and careful in saying anything about himself as he was about getting confessions. Sometimes I felt like shaking him until all his thoughts spilled out of his head. Mama would tell me everything. She'd wake me up in the middle of the night to tell me her dreams when she had a real fascinating one, like the time she grew wings. She could fly all over Tucumsett Parish, but no matter how far she flew, she'd circle back and sit on my windowsill to watch me sleep. Papa never told me anything about his dreams.

I kept going, hoping I'd feel better soon. "And I wanted to know why you'd help a lady out of her car."

"I help Mrs. Mabel out of the car."

"But Mrs. Mabel's an old widow."

Papa smiled and I knew I'd just made a confession. He patted my hand. "You're really wondering why a married man like me would be helping a lady out of her car?"

"Yes."

"We're just friends, Nissa." He patted my shoulder. "How about pickle sandwiches?"

"Fine." I sure was glad I loved pickle sandwiches as much as Papa or I'd go hungry five times out of ten. Papa was always making those darn things. But when it came to Miss Ross, I felt it was him who had a confession to make. And he proved me right by inviting her to our house not more than three weeks later.

It was a Saturday just before October rolled into November. I was in the front hall polishing the table. Mama loved to see her wavy reflection in the polished wood. As I stood there rubbing, I half hoped I'd see Mama's face come shining back at me if I polished long enough. Miss Lara Ross came onto the porch hanging on the arm of Mr. Jonah Hess. Mr. Hess was a big man who had to turn sideways to get through the door of a single-seat outhouse. He had red hair that stuck straight up in a rooster tail right above his forehead whether it was short or long, so he kept it short to make it look like he made the hair stand up on purpose. The thing I found fascinating about him was the deep crease in the bridge of his nose. He once told me he got it in a logging accident. I wondered if it was a cut that went clean through to the bone. It must have hurt something fierce.

Old Jonah was laughing as they came to the screen door. Miss Lara was laughing, too, showing off her dentist-cleaned teeth. She got them cleaned free on account of her uncle was the dentist. They were always so white and shiny you'd think she used bleach for mouthwash. As usual, she wore her black hair pulled back into a big barrette that hung at the base of her neck.

Papa met them at the door. They were all smiles and hellos. Adults are so phony—you'd think they were all auditioning for a picture show. Miss Lara Ross was no Claudette Colbert. And although he had a cleft chin and a deep voice, Papa wasn't Clark Gable. Grandma Dee always said my mama's biggest problem was that she never learned to be polite. I say she was the most genuine adult I've known. I'll take honesty over politeness any day.

Papa and his visitors stepped into the hall. Lara wiggled her fingers at me and kind of bowed her head in my direction. Damn if she wasn't wearing gloves again. Navy blue this time to match her dress. She couldn't even wave. She had to waggle her fingers at me like I was a pet-shop puppy.

"We're going to listen to the radio, Neesay," Papa said, holding his hand out to guide the others into the parlor while he looked at me. "Care to join us?"

Listen to the radio? It was Mama's radio. She'd washed and ironed other people's shirts, frocks, and pants for three months to pay for it. What right did they have to listen to it? Miss Lara Ross hadn't stood over a hot iron until her hair curled into frizzy little coils around her face and blisters popped up at the base of every finger on her right hand.

"No thank you," I said. I never did learn to say what I was feeling, like Mama. I guess I take after Papa in that regard.

They went into the parlor. I heard the low voices of the radio. They made me think there were men inside talking through the cone of a gramophone. When she taught me how to dance on Friday nights, Mama used to magnify her voice by speaking through the cone of our gramophone like the barkers at the county fair.

The hotel down the street had a dance every Friday night. Mr. Cassell, the owner, charged 75¢ to get in, so Papa could afford it only once a month. On the nights he didn't take Mama dancing, Papa used the time to proof articles for the weekly paper.

Mama worked too, but she normally had five jobs in a month because she couldn't keep one. Her own father, Grandpa Jared, says it's 'cause she's flighty. Mama said it was because people never wanted to see things from her point of view. When she picked cotton for Peter Journiette, she sang to give herself a rhythm to pace her work, but she was fired for "acting like a darky." After Mr. Journiette said that to her, Mama poisoned his well with black shoe polish. He made sure Mama didn't pick cotton for anybody in Tucumsett Parish again.

When she did other people's laundry, she hung the clothes from the line beside our house, whether she was cleaning blankets or underpants. The bachelor Thibodeaux brothers who run the feed store across the street were the first to refuse her services after they saw their undergarments flapping in the breeze where anyone walking down Main Street could see them. Mama figured everyone knew men wore underpants. As she said, "What was there to hide in an empty pair of underpants?"

She lost her job in the post office when she started telling people about how Miss Chessie Roubidoux read their letters. That job lasted only two days. She tried selling sandwiches on the train, but the railroad kicked her off when she tried to sell to whites and blacks alike. Mama said she didn't know what the scientists were talking about when they said some men can't see colors. She'd never met a man who was color blind. They all saw the difference between black and white skin. Except for Papa. He had never even talked down to a Negro man. In fact, he calls our blacksmith Mr. Vincent, not "boy" as the other men in town do. I call him Mr. Vincent, too, and he made me a set of jacks out of horseshoe nails.

The truth was there was no one in town who saw things Mama's way except for me. Even Papa had a hard time seeing the things that Mama did with her clear eye. He wouldn't let her help with the newspaper after she misprinted the title of a story so it read, "Harper Welcomes its Newest Bayor" instead of "Harper Welcomes its Newest Mayor." He didn't agree that Mayor Kinley resembled a hound dog baying at the moon when he gave his speeches.

Mama was like a bird trapped in a woman's body. On the Friday nights she'd stay home, she'd wear her gauzy dress. It was the faintest lavender—so pale it looked white in the moonlight. It was loose and flowing so it floated up like feathers in the wind when she danced. There was a scarf attached at the neck that hung down her arms, and she could hold the ends of the fabric between her fingers and raise them up like wings. There was a big, old tear down the back of the dress, but she'd never say how it got there.

I remember our last Friday that May. She'd put her dress on and put ribbons in my hair. She'd said, "Won't be long now. When you turn twelve we can take your hair out of braids and start curling it."

She took off my braid ties, ran her fingers through my hair, pulled it down to its full length where it grazed my shoulders, then twirled a lock of it up on a finger. "Tsss," she hissed when her finger was up close to my scalp, and I giggled.

She wiggled her finger loose, then opened the doors to the balcony and let the music drift in. She held her arms out and started to sway. I ran up to her in my bare feet.

She took my hands in hers. Her hands were cool and strong. Mama rarely sweat and she could break a stick thicker than my wrist without using her knee. She could also glide when she danced. Sometimes I'd sit at the end of her bed and watch as she flowed with the music, her arms raised in the air turning with her as she waltzed in front of the open windows. To me, she was the Isadora Duncan of Louisiana—all grace, beauty, and bare feet twirling away to the waltzing tune of Gideon Kelly's fiddle.

I watched her until I couldn't stand being still any longer, then we'd dance until her toes were too sore to go on. I was always stomping on them. She tried to teach me to dance, but I just wanted to hop on her feet and fly like she did when she went flitting around as if her bones were hollow.

When my lesson was over, she took up the cone—our gramophone didn't work, the crank was stuck. "Ladies and gentlemen, prepare yourselves. An important guest will be arriving soon." Her voice boomed and made the insides of my ears feel heavy. Lowering the cone, she whispered, "Better get ready, my duchess. The people are waiting."

That was my cue to hightail it to her closet. I ran in and picked the dress with the embroidered wild violets. It's my favorite because Grandma Dee had sewn it so it only came to Mama's knees which made it floor length on me. I wasn't tripping over the hem when I came out of Mama's closet with her pearls hanging around my neck and crocodile-skin heels on my feet. I waltzed out of her closet like I was going to a palace for a dance—without a prince. I'd show the royalty there how to square dance without the help of a prince.

Mama dropped her straw hat on my head as she raised the cone to her mouth: "Ladies and gentlemen, please welcome the Grand Duchess Nissa of Skein." Skein's the logging town Papa's family's from. It's a cold, muddy place with log houses illuminated by fireplaces and lumber men who went into the tall, dark pines before the gray fog lifted over their knotty trunks, but it sounded good when Mama said it through the cone. She clapped her hands and made the sound of cheers in the back of her throat. We laughed.

She dropped the cone, then scooped me up and swung me around by the arms so my legs flew up in the air and her dress fanned out like a flag in the wind. She pulled me in and we sank to the floor, laughing. I pulled my hair out of my mouth, then did the same for Mama. She rubbed my tummy saying, "I see you walk around in my clothes and for a second, I'm sure I've shrunk."

I loved it when she said that. Mama's beautiful. I want to be able to float across the floor and walk downtown with no shoes on my feet. If I was just like her, I would be able to cook and iron my own clothes and pick up and leave whenever I wanted to.

Would that mean I didn't love Papa anymore? Would I do baby making? No. I didn't want that part of Mama's life. She didn't really want it either. She wanted to be right here with me and Papa. That Sawdust Man took her away. Kidnapped her, I bet. My mama wouldn't get tired of us. She couldn't wait to come home. I was sure of it. Papa should have sent the sheriff after that man.

Garden Fire

I WAS DREAMING ABOUT MAMA WHEN I HEARD THE SCREEN
door shut. I looked up to see Mr. Hess's wide back as he
walked away. I knew he'd just been an escort for Miss Lara
Ross because the people in town think no self-respecting
woman would walk to a man's house alone. Not Mama.
She'd be quick to point out that Miss Ross would still be
alone in that house, our house, with a man, a married man
at that. I was so mad, I thought of serving them lemonade
with salt in it. I could pretend the lemons were Miss Ross's
sourpuss face and squeeze them until all the juice came out
and she was shriveled up like a witch. I could feel the lemon
juice on my fingers when Papa came into the hall saying,
"How about giving Miss Lara a tour of the garden, Nissa?"

No way, I thought. Those are me and Mama's flowers.
No glove-wearing husband chaser was going to go stomping
about in our garden. A nasty thought got hold of me. What
if the Sawdust Man was married? Was Mama taking a papa
away from some other child? I didn't want to think about it.
To think about it would mean I really believed it in some
way and my mama would never steal a little girl's papa.

Besides, I had more important things to do—like protect Mama's garden from the glove-wearing fingers of Miss Lara Ross. I ran out the back door to lead the way into the garden, shouting, "Mama's roses have new growth!"

Papa and Miss Ross stepped out after me. When I looked back, Miss Ross was resting her arm on Papa's. She probably thought it looked like she needed support to keep from falling, but I knew she was flirting. Like I said, she's lousy at it.

At least the garden is all fenced in and no one could see them. Mrs. Dayton across the alley was sure to be talking up a hurricane at church if she saw Papa waltzing through his garden with another woman. I wouldn't even put it past that woman to watch from an upstairs window just to get a sight of someone in our family doing something wrong. She'd done it before. I'd heard her telling Mrs. Minkie over at the mercantile that Mama did her gardening in her nightclothes if she had a mind to. Mrs. Dayton thought it was sinful. I think it's cool and comfortable to wear a gauzy cotton nightdress in the suffocating heat of Louisiana. The nightdress hangs loose on your body and lets the air get to your skin. Besides, I love to watch the white fabric drag through the flowers. The whiteness makes their petals seem brighter, the reds redder, the blues bluer.

Old Man Beauregard next to us never did anything except bury coffee tins in his backyard. Nobody would listen to anything he said about other people's strange habits. I don't think Mr. Beauregard is strange, he's just scared. He's the only Negro that owns a house in Harper proper. His grandfather built the place and the Klan came more than once to push their family out, taking all their belongings and threatening to burn the place. He buries his valuables in those coffee cans and I can't say I blame him. The only problem is, he's got his house money underground, so he ends up doing a lot of digging come bill-paying time. If I knew he wouldn't mind other folks knowing where his treasures are hid, I'd offer to help, but as things are, I stay inside our brick garden walls mostly.

The walls that kept us safe from the neighborhood were made out of what I call field rocks. They're the rounded and grainy kind that have to be picked out of the fields. They only come in different shades of brown and gray, but the rocks I like in the garden are the flagstones that are buried to make a path from the back door to the gate. They come in colors that pull you in—like the deepest green a green can be, and a purply red that prompted Mama to wonder if someone had murdered chickens on that stone and left the blood there to soak in. The flagstones were smooth to the touch and rippled like the waves on a lake when there was only a faint breeze blowing.

I ran down the path. "I'll show you Mama's roses."

"She's so proud of her mother's purple roses," Papa said with a laugh. He loved to watch Mama work in the garden, her skirts tied in knots at her knees, her feet black with dirt, her hands moving as swift as a hummingbird's wings—clipping here, pulling there, then stopping long enough to feel the silky texture of the petals. Yet, here he was, parading through the garden with a strange lady. Why would he bring her into my mother's garden? I wanted to kick her out, throw tiny stones at her until she fled.

"Purple?" Miss Ross asked. "How exotic. You must have paid a pretty penny for those."

Papa touched a green bud on the rosebush. I could tell he was longing for Mama. "Heirah loved the beauty of these roses. They have a purple color so deep it makes a red rose look pale." He smiled, then blushed, saying, "Besides, you buy the bare roots and they grow forever. It was a good investment."

Miss Ross looked at all the rosebushes, then said, "Looks like they're getting ready to bloom again."

"Mama cut them back this spring so they'll grow back even thicker," I said before Papa could say anything. I didn't want Miss Ross to know Mama had cut the flowers off when she left. That would tell her Mama did it so we couldn't see her flowers while she was away. I missed her more without her roses here. It was a mean thing for Mama to do and I didn't want anyone to know Mama could be mean. People already said too many bad things about her.

Besides, Miss Ross had no idea what kind of a gardener my mama was. She'd probably never even seen a purple rose before, and Mama had a whole bed of them. In fact, Mama had started our garden from the ground up. When we moved here after Benjamin died, the garden was a tangled, brown, knee-high jungle.

Papa had looked at the weeds and sighed. "Such a waste," he'd said, carrying a box of linens into the dining room. Mama didn't believe in waste. She dipped orange rinds into sugar and ate them instead of throwing them away and she burned the garden the first night we were there. She didn't want anything to go to waste, but she left Papa and me. Didn't she know we'd go to waste without her?

"Do you help your mother with her gardening, Nissa?" Miss Ross asked, bending down to touch the petal of a ruby-dot hibiscus. She didn't even take her glove off then!

"Sometimes," I said, sitting down on a wooden bench under our cherry tree.

Papa escorted Miss Ross to the other bench saying, "Nissa's in here every day. She knows more about gardens than any eleven-year-old knows about doll clothes."

Miss Ross hummed, pretending she was interested, but she wasn't. Neither was I. I was dream-remembering about the fire. Mama calls remembering *dream-remembering* because you never remember things as they were. You change things with the same fancy you use when you dream.

Papa sat next to Miss Ross on the bench across from me and I watched to see if he touched her hand. I smiled when I realized the gloves made it so he couldn't trace the veins of her hands, as he had done with Mama. He talked to her in a whisper about all the different flowers in the garden—from the tongue-pink azalea bushes bordering the house to the blood-red bougainvillea crawling over the wall to peek at Mr. Beauregard. She pointed to the ruby-dot hibiscus and said they were pretty. Pretty! How boring. As Mama says, they're little Asian girls with their tiny white painted faces staring out at us with their red eyes full of interest. They were like faces crawling out of the earth on stems to reach toward the sun. Mama even planted Rose-of-Sharon hibiscus between the ruby-dot girls, so the big purple flowers could act as parasols until she snipped them for hibiscus tea.

I couldn't listen to Papa and Miss Ross with their silly

flirting anymore. My mind returned to Mama when she'd set fire to the garden. I remember her telling Aunt Sarah all about it when Sarah finally came down from Virginia last year. I watched them from the back steps as they walked out into the garden, arm in arm. Mama with her skirts in knots, her feet bare, and Aunt Sarah stepping gingerly from rock to rock in clickety heels.

"Ivar thinks I've lost my head," Mama said with a laugh. "I was just following Dr. Swenson's orders. He said the best thing I could do was start over with a clean slate."

"But a fire, Heirah? You could have been hurt."

"Well, I could also slip getting out of the tub, break my head open, and bleed to death. Shall I stop bathing?"

"No, but you could have hoed everything under to clean out the flower beds."

"There's nothing cleaner than fire. Ash is the purest substance on earth."

"Where did you get such nonsense?"

"My science book!" I shouted from the steps.

Aunt Sarah covered her mouth in embarrassment when she realized I was listening, but Mama looked over her shoulder at me with a smile. Mama told Sarah, "Nissa and I are getting an education together."

Sarah shook her head. "And neither one of you has any common sense."

Mama pressed her lips together. She was mad. "I'd rather be happy than common."

"Nissa!" Papa's shout brought me back to the garden.

He pointed to Mama's purple rosebush, asking, "What's their name again?"

"Cardinal Richelieu."

"Really?" Miss Ross gasped. "Wasn't he the counsel to a king of France?" She was actually impressed, not that I cared. I knew Papa only asked to get me involved in the conversation, but I wasn't interested. Staring at the flame-red bougainvillea taking over the garden wall, I remembered the fire that had devoured the brown, twisted weeds of the garden.

I was upstairs when Mama started the fire. I'd been setting my dolls up to show them our new room. I stood up from sitting Charlotte the one-eyed bear in her wicker chair and saw the flames blazing in my window.

They were only a reflection, but I thought there was a fireball spinning through the night, charging to burn me up for forgetting to put Grandma Nissa's silver slotted spoon in the crate when I'd helped Mama pack the silverware. Seeing the flames grow larger, I screamed and Papa went running, but he was yelling for Mama, not me. Thinking the fire was threatening Mama, I'd followed him.

Fire danced through the garden. The flower beds were a carpet of flames as the fire swept up to the top of the dried sunflower stalks, then leapt onto the tangled remains of the ivy along the garden wall. Sparks flew through the air like evil rain. Mama sat in the crook of a tree, teasing the flames with water she splashed from a bucket in her lap. Papa said she was crazy and yelled at her to get down. Mama jumped. When I saw her skirts blow upward, I thought she was flying and feared the fire would burn her wings. The glow of the fire made the fabric of her skirt shine like a moth's wings as it flutters in the light of a lantern. I expected the flames to catch Mama's skirt with their lashing tongues and devour her, but she landed barefoot on the boulder by the fountain, untouched by the fire and laughing as if she were playing a game of chase.

Papa was beating down the fire with a linen tablecloth soaked in water. He'd taken it from the pile of wet blankets Mama had left on the path. Mama helped him, slapping back the fire with a blanket. I hid behind the door, praying the fire wouldn't burn my parents.

When the ground was covered in an ash darker than wet soil, smoke hung in the air like fog and the fire was nothing more than a sizzling sound that made me think of hissing snakes buried in the earth. Mama stomped past me, shouting back to Papa, "Where's it going to go? The walls are stone!"

Papa stormed in after her. "You could've torched the house."

Like the fire, Mama jumped from one place to the next. Papa was worried about the house, but she flew right to a whole other idea. She planted her hands on her hips like a *Ladies' Home Journal* model, then said, "I could also pack up and leave."

This was the first time I'd ever heard Mama threaten to leave. If she really meant what she said that night, then she'd been ready to leave even when I was three years old. Mama turned at the bottom of the stairs to face Papa. Her cheeks were red under the soot and she was smiling as she said, "Would you like that?"

"Heirah." Papa said her name as if he were sighing when he was sad.

* * *

I was thinking about how sad Papa looked when Mama talked about leaving, then Miss Ross interrupted my dream by asking, "What are you thinking?"

I looked up at Miss Ross and saw that her eyes were blue and shiny like Mary Carroll's favorite doll. I thought of stealing the feather from her hat and using it to poke her in the eye, then I noticed we were alone. "Where's Papa?"

"He went inside to get some lemonade."

She really should have said that he went inside to leave us alone. Papa probably believed it was actually possible for me to welcome a strange woman into my mother's garden. I didn't want her pointy toes anywhere near Mama's flowers. I wanted her out. I wanted her gone. I hoped she'd die.

"You looked so lost in your thoughts." Miss Ross smiled with her lips together. She looked kind of sweet without all her teeth showing. "What were you thinking about?"

"Fires."

"Fires?" Miss Ross raised a gloved hand to her lips. I really hated those smooth, navy blue gloves with the white bows at the wrists. They made me feel like I was betraying Mama by looking at them, by being there with Miss Ross and staring at her prissy gloves.

I stood up and started down the path. Passing by the buds of Mama's silky purple roses, I longed to smell them. In full bloom, their scent was so sweet it made me dizzy. But they were still closed up so the smell would be faint and distant, just like Mama.

I bent down and picked a Rose-of-Sharon instead. Their smell was sweet, too, but their tea was better. I loved the way their petals melted into the water and turned it violet.

Twirling the flower, I watched the deep purple center spin like a dark eye as I told Miss Ross, "Mama burned all the dead things in the garden to make the soil rich and black so she could plant things. I was thinking about the fire."

"That must have been dangerous—a fire so close to the house."

Miss Ross was all scared and nervous at the thought of Mama's fire, but she didn't seem to mind trying to warm up to Papa. I wanted to give her a little heat. I could start her hat on fire and, before she had time to blink, it'd burn its way right down to those ugly gloves.

Papa came out onto the steps with the lemonade. "Here we are."

Miss Ross laughed nervously, then followed Papa to the benches. Her hand shook when she picked up a glass.

"What's the matter?"

"Oh," she blushed, "Nissa just told me about the fire. I guess I'm a little spooked."

"I know it scared me." Papa forced a smile.

I watched Papa look at her with his head tilted to one side. She was going on and on about how dangerous fires could be. It was obvious Miss Ross would've sided with Papa about the fire Mama had started. I was suddenly worried he might like her. Maybe even more than Mama. She wouldn't set a fire in her garden or suck on sugar-coated orange rinds. She probably wouldn't let me wear her dresses nor dance with me on Friday nights. I hated her. Even if I liked her, she wasn't and would never be my mother.

All Hallow's Eve

THE ONLY GOOD THING ABOUT THE WHOLE MONTH OF October that year was Halloween. It was my second favorite holiday next to Christmas. Mama said she appreciated the day on account of the fact that she considered herself a bit of a restless soul. You see, Halloween started out as All Hallow's Eve—a time to celebrate the dead. Folks back in Europe would bring food to their dead relatives and pray to God to put restless souls at ease. Some folks dressed up as scary monsters because when there's all that communicating with the dead, sometimes the evil dead come back and you've got to scare them away.

That's how it all got started. The food people gave to the dead became candy given to little kids who were dressed up like monsters because it was fun, not because there's really evil spirits walking the earth. At least, none that I've ever seen.

Simon Carroll was always trying to change that. Every Halloween we all snuck out to the old abandoned church on Charleston Road. Mrs. Carroll thought we went to the Halloween party at the hotel. She would've tanned us all good if she knew we were telling ghost stories in an old church. Halloween was an evil holiday in her mind and she would just as soon keep all her children home, but Mr. Carroll liked to have the evening alone with her, so she let the kids go to the dance at the hotel if they didn't wear costumes.

I didn't wear a costume so Mary wouldn't feel bad and Papa knew we went out to the old church because I told him. I guess he could have told Mrs. Carroll, but I don't think they got along all that well seeing as how they felt about each other's children. Papa trusted Simon though, so he knew I was safe.

He was wrong. Simon was evil. He'd bring a flashlight and shine it up on his face as he told ghost stories in a voice that made it sound like he was speaking from an echoey crypt. That Halloween, he started talking about an evil man who came round every so often to lure restless women away. He never looked the same to any two people. To one girl he'd be short with a freckled face. To a young woman, he'd arrive in a suit and have clear blue eyes and a cleft chin. He'd promise her the moon, then walk her straight off the face of the earth.

I imagined I saw Mama watching a man walk out of the darkness of the north end of Main Street. He carried his hat in his hand. His suit was sprinkled with sawdust that shone in the moonlight. He smiled and promised Mama . . . What could he promise her?

Simon said, "One woman who lost her baby heard it crying in the dark. When she went out into the night to find it, the man was cradling the baby in his arms. When she held it, it turned to glass." Teddy laughed and Little Anthony buried his face in Mary's shawl. I felt myself emptying out. What if the Sawdust Man was really an evil spirit who lured Mama away by promising to bring Bennie back?

"He isn't real is he, Simon?" I needed to hear him say it. Maybe it was the wind blowing through the chinks in the walls or the way the moon cast reaching shadows of a dead tree across the floor that softened my mind, but I believed that evil man was real. He was real and he'd taken my mama away.

"Of course." Simon nodded. "That's what happened to Mabel Lathum."

Mabel Lathum disappeared the night before her wedding when I was just a wee girl. Everyone had stories about how she walked in her sleep and was carried off by the river or eaten by wild beasts.

I stood up shouting, "No, it isn't true!" I couldn't bear the thought of Mama in an evil man's grip. It was making me crumble inside.

"Sure it is. I've even seen him once or twice myself, slipping between gravestones." Simon laughed.

I screamed, "No it isn't!"

"You're scaring her, Simon!" Mary shouted.

Teddy said, "She looks like she's going to wet herself."

I was going to explode if someone didn't prove to me right then and there that no such man existed. "Stop it! Tell me the truth!"

"He's real, Nissa. And I hear he's back in town tonight, looking for motherless girls." Simon said it without even cracking a smile. I wanted to jump right through the window if it would get me out of there fast. I ran for the door. Mary screamed for me to stop, but it just scared me even more.

I ran across the open fields, afraid to enter the woods, screaming for Mama. I was out of my head—believing the evil man was out there watching me, maybe even following me as I ran for home. I had to reach Papa. He had to get Mama back. I begged God to make Mama safe.

As I turned down Main Street, I saw Papa running toward me. I knew then and there that it was true, Mama had been taken. I fell to the ground in despair.

Papa dropped down next to me, "What is it, Nissa?" He gathered me into his arms.

I clung to him, screaming, "Mama's gone. He took her. He took her!"

Papa patted me, saying, "Shh, it's okay. Don't believe any awful stories. Your mama's just fine. See." He waved a letter in front of me.

"Mama!" I grabbed the letter and ripped it open. I couldn't read a word in the dark. I screamed in frustration, then there was a light over my shoulder. I didn't look back, I just read the note.

Happy Halloween, Nissa!

I loved the way she made the extra curly-cue on the bottom of each *s* when she wrote my name.

Just a note to let you know this
restless soul is loving you from afar.
  Love,
  Mama

"Love, Mama," I read aloud. I looked back thinking Papa was holding the lamp for me, but it was Miss Lara Ross, smiling away like I was reading a Christmas card from her folks.

I got up and walked to the house. I was so happy to know that Mama was well and loving me, but mad that Miss Ross had to be there to see it. She was a bad person, running after another woman's husband like she was. Something had to be done about her, but for the time being, I was just happy to know Mama was all right. But she didn't want me to know where she was. She didn't put an address on the envelope, just her name, Heirah Rae—not even a Bergen.

What to Do
with Bad People

MAMA KNEW WHAT TO DO ABOUT BAD PEOPLE. WHEN I WAS five, our milkman moved away. The man who took his place was Mr. Rainey. He was a bachelor who delivered milk in the morning, then hauled feed in the afternoon so he could raise enough money to buy a house for the woman he loved, Frances Journiette. He'd do anything for money, including stealing our weekly paper and selling it on his milk route. Mama let it pass when he took our first Saturday paper. As she put it, "If Mr. Rainey needs a little extra money to buy something nice for Frances, I won't keep it from her."

But Mr. Rainey took advantage of her kindness and stole our paper a second week in a row, so Mama put on her leather gardening gloves, then rubbed itch weed all over the necks of our empty milk bottles. I saw Mr. Rainey in church that Sunday scratching away, like all his sins were itching their way into his fingertips and he was clawing them out.

The following Friday, Mama left a note that said,

Take our paper again and
it won't be your hands that
are itching tomorrow.

-H-

Mama tacked a pair of his underpants to our porch right next to the note. That was when Mama was still doing people's laundry and Mr. Rainey was one of her customers. He didn't steal any more of our newspapers and Mama seemed right proud.

Mama went to such lengths to save our paper because it was real important. It was Mama's way of catching up on all the goings-on around town. Plus, Papa helped Mr. Hess make each paper in their office over the mercantile. Papa put the pages together by setting tiny letter blocks into wooden trays to make headlines like, *"The New Deal, Old News," Says Sen. Long*, or *Huey to Share His Wealth All the Way to the White House*. He covered the letters with ink, then pressed paper down over the letters to create pages of the newspaper. When all the papers were printed and dry, Papa would walk one over to our house. If the front door was closed, that meant Mama was still sleeping; so Papa would roll up the paper, then slip it in the handle.

After Mr. Rainey took to stealing our paper, Mama never slept in. She was in the kitchen when Papa came, ready to take the paper from his ink-stained hand. She'd give him a kiss. They'd laugh, then Papa would eat one of the sweet rolls Mama would have ready for him on the stove. He'd take others back to the office for the delivery boys, but he'd always eat his on the front porch before he left. I'd sit on the porch to eat one with him. When I watched him lick the frosting off his inky fingers, I could almost feel the acidy taste of ink in my mouth, but he didn't seem to notice it. Papa loved his sweet rolls.

And Mama loved the paper. She liked to lay the whole paper out in the downstairs hallway in the morning, before the heat started to curl the hairs around her face. She'd open the doors to the garden so she could hear the birds singing and let the smell of the flowers and the dirt drift in. She said she liked the roses and columbines for breakfast best, and she meant it. I've seen her eat rose petals on a rainy day because their smell didn't reach the house on account of the rain.

Once she had the garden doors open, she'd open the front door, leave the screen door closed, then pull down the shade she'd fashioned out of an old blue bedspread. Then she would begin to read the paper. She always knew it was time to stop reading when the sun got high enough to shine through the shade and cast blue shadows on the pages.

With the doors open, she'd have to weigh each sheet down with a rock on the top corner. She'd collected a pile of rocks of a size that fit inside her fist while weeding in the garden, then polished them to a shine so they'd catch the sun as they sat on the pantry windowsill when they weren't weighing her paper down.

There were enough pages to cover the floor all the way from the kitchen door to the parlor door at the other end of the hallway that runs down the center of our house. When the pages were spread out and weighed down with her polished rocks, Mama would plop down on her belly like a fish returning to water. She'd lean on her elbows with her bare feet swinging in the air and read out loud.

She'd start by the front door, then work her way to the garden. Newspapers aren't like books, so the stories didn't stay together when she took it all apart. That didn't bother Mama. She'd read to the bottom of a page, then crawl up to the next one and make the stories connect somehow. An article about the Gadseys' blue-ribbon tomatoes turned into a burglary report. A list of the women in the quilting bee down in Gainesburg ended with Edward Journiette Taylor, seventy-five, who was survived by his brother, Stephen Taylor, his three sons, fourteen grandchildren, and five great-grandchildren. She always said, "Mixing things up makes these people's lives seem more exciting than they'll ever be."

When she really liked how the mixed articles worked out, she'd cut them out, then paste them together in her scrapbook of the articles Papa wrote. Her favorite combination was, "Black man, about to be lynched . . . gets medal for bravery and is honored with a feast by his home town."

She'd slap the paper, then say, "That's the way it should be."

Mama would crawl over the pages until her clothes were black with ink and she knew all there was to know about Tucumsett Parish. You see, Mama had to learn what she knew about the Parish from the paper because not too many folks talked to her. They thought she was crazy for sitting on the roof on hot summer nights when she couldn't sleep. Mama would pull a shawl over her shoulders, then walk right out onto the roof. We had big, taller-than-Papa windows, so she could step up on the sill, then waltz right onto the shingles covering our porch. Sitting with her knees pulled up to her chest, she'd stare up at the stars and let the late-night breezes cool her off.

Back before I had to get up for school in the morning, Mama would take me out there after midnight. I remember her pointing to a cluster of stars in a part of the sky that seemed kind of purple. "Doesn't that look like one of our roses, Nissa?"

I imagined the deep purple petals opening to reveal a star in the center of a rosebud. Mama could always make me think of magical things. I let my chin sink to say yes as I stared up at the stars.

She took a deep breath, then told me, "Louisiana's a place that begs decent people to live at night. Nothing cools off until all the gossipers have stopped blowing their hot air and gone to sleep. Decent people can sit out on their porches and admire God's handiwork."

Mama didn't like the townspeople any more than they liked her. She hated how they watched us and told people what we were doing, like Clem Thibodeaux had with the laundry—and he hadn't stopped there. He was always up pacing the floor in his room over the feed store. We could see him passing in front of the windows, his shadow cast onto his roof like a puppet made from fingers held up in front of a lantern. Mama figured he was too ornery to sleep. As she saw it, mean people didn't sleep because they were haunted by bad dreams. Mama said bad dreams come from two things—bad things on their way or sins returning to take their ransom from your soul. So in Mama's book, if you did something wrong, don't go to sleep until you'd asked God for forgiveness.

Clem never did ask God for forgiveness, I suppose, because he always had big bags under his eyes and spent more time pacing than he did anything else, except maybe tattling on Mama like a schoolboy. It wasn't but a day after our stargazing on the roof of the porch that Mrs. Minkie had a word with Mama about it. We were in the mercantile picking out fabric to send to Grandma Dee so she could sew me a new dress for Easter. We were admiring a cotton broadcloth the same color as the peach azaleas in our front yard when Mrs. Minkie came over. She stood across the cutting table from Mama and said, "Mr. Thibodeaux says you've been sitting on your roof again, Heirah."

"What I do on my roof is my affair."

"Not when you bring a child out there with you."

"What my child does is her affair."

I didn't dare even breathe. I could see Mama gripping the cloth in her fists. I was afraid she'd haul off and hit Mrs. Minkie and get kicked out of the store. A tiny part of me was embarrassed that Mama would talk back like that when I knew ladies were supposed to respect what was proper— at least that's what Mrs. Owens always said. I was also scared. Mama was powerful. She could reach inside you and squeeze your heart with anger just by looking at you. I didn't want anybody to feel that anger. Not even Mrs. Minkie—the nose of Harper.

Mrs. Minkie said, "Some people would say that good parents are intensely concerned with their children's actions."

Then Mama came back with, "Well, I don't listen to some people. I raise my child as I see fit."

"Of course." Mrs. Minkie forced a smile, but her eyes were squinting as if she were scowling.

I was instantly proud. Mama did what she felt was right. When I thought back to what she had said to Mrs. Minkie, I realized she wanted me to do the same thing. Mama wasn't the type to let other people tell her what was right and wrong.

Still, people were always trying to tell Mama what not to do. They were especially upset with her decision to join the women's group in Gainesburg. Mrs. Linzy said it was against the Bible to protest women's servitude to their husbands. Mrs. Linzy even said to Mama right in the foyer of the church, "After all, Mrs. Bergen, the Bible says in Ephesians, chapter five, verse twenty-two, 'Wives, submit yourself unto your husbands, as unto the Lord.'"

Mama had smiled, then said, "You're right and the prophet John says following Jesus is the Truth and the Truth shall set you free and Jesus showed us what that freedom meant. After all, there wasn't a rabble-rouser any better than Jesus."

We walked out of the church before Mrs. Linzy could open her mouth again. Mama sat smiling in the front seat of our old car, Betsy. I crawled in next to her and Papa joined us saying, "You're sure to have Madge Linzy flipping through the book of John tonight."

They giggled and I laughed, too, because I thought I was supposed to, but it didn't make much sense to me. I didn't understand half the stuff Mama did with her group from

Gainesburg, but I know they went all the way to Kentucky in a truck before I was born to be with their Kentucky sisters when women got the right to vote on who becomes mayor or president.

Mama even voted for herself when we had an election for the mayor of Harper back when I was eight. We were all in the veterans' hall when they were announcing the votes. Mr. Cassell was reading off the results because he was the unofficial chairman of the election on account of the fact that he'd hosted the Welcome to Being Mayor Party at his hotel. He'd stood behind a podium with a bow tie that looked like it'd been drawn on his shirt. Smiling, he'd said, "Before I announce the election results, I'd like to point out that a young woman in our community received a vote. It appears from the penmanship on this ballot that Heirah Rae Bergen voted for herself." There was such a ruckus of laughter and hissing I thought I'd wandered into a cockfight. Mama sat there with her head up and her eyes fixed on Mr. Cassell. She wasn't going to let him embarrass her. Papa didn't even blink as he sat down beside her. Trouble is, I don't know if he was in shock or showing his support.

Either way, the town wasn't impressed. Chessie Roubidoux even walked right up to Mama at Mr. Cassell's party, then said, "Forgive me for being blunt, Heirah, but you have quite the gall to think you can run a town when you can't even run a decent household."

Mama looked Chessie in the eye, then said, "My personal affairs aside, I haven't met a man yet who gave a tinker's dam what happened to this town as long as the Negroes stayed out and the women stayed pregnant."

Chessie Roubidoux's hand went up as if she were about to swat a fly away from her face, but she brought it back and slapped Mama across the cheek. Miss Roubidoux's never been married, so she gets real angry when people say *pregnant* in public. I was ready to push Miss Roubidoux into the nearest mud puddle, but Mama laughed. There was a bright red palm mark on the side of her face, and everyone in the room was staring at her, but Mama just laughed. I wanted to hide under the nearest table, but then I saw Papa. He was standing by the bar with a glass of water in his hand, looking at Mama. The glass of water sunk down as Papa lowered his hand and closed his eyes, as if he were in pain. He hurt for Mama when she couldn't do it for herself. I suppose that meant he loved her.

Mama may not have shown that Miss Roubidoux's slap bothered her in the least bit, but Mama fixed that old witch just the same. She went to the quilting bee the very next week and sewed Miss Chessie's skirt to the bottom side of the quilt. Mama knew just what to do with bad people.

She would have known what to do to keep Miss Ross away from Papa before they got any big baby-making ideas. Mixing up a batch of cornmeal pancakes, I tried to think of just how Mama would get rid of Miss Ross. I couldn't have that glove-wearing lady taking over my mama's house.

I could rub poison oak in her gloves, but she never took them off. Maybe I could invite her over to help me sew up the tear in my favorite dress, then sew it right to hers. That was a bad idea. It would ruin my dress.

Papa came in as I was melting butter in the skillet.

"Making breakfast?" he asked, as he read over my math assignment.

"Cornmeal pancakes with bacon grease, as good as Mama's."

"You do your sums like your mother, too," he smiled. "You need to do this over again, Neesay; you've got over half of them wrong."

"Are you saying Mama's stupid?" I shook the wooden spoon I held and splattered Papa with butter.

"No," Papa said, wiping his shirt off with a towel. "I merely meant that she wasn't good at math."

"She can read faster than you and sew and cook and paint better than anyone in Tucumsett Parish!"

"Come here." Papa sat down and opened his arms to me. I didn't want to go to him. He was talking trash about Mama just like everyone else. It made me ache for Mama. He patted his lap, then said again, "Come here."

I didn't move, so he got up and walked over to me. Pulling up the step stool, he sat down in front of me. "Neesay, your mother is a wonderful woman and she is good at all those things. I didn't mean to say anything bad about her. She would be the first person to say she didn't know how to do sums."

He was right. Mama used to say the only people who needed to know how to multiply were bankers and store owners; everybody else had fingers and trust for that sort of thing.

"Well, she's a real good mama."

Papa pulled me close. "She is the best mama she knows how to be."

"The best mama in the world," I said, but Papa didn't answer. He didn't believe it and I hated him for that.

Papa was the reason I knew everything was all right. If Mama said it was okay to walk along the rail when there was no train in sight and Papa agreed, then I knew I was safe. When Mama tried to tell me we could make our own balloon out of a camping tent, a laundry basket, and helium from the circus, I wanted to believe her. I wanted to soar into the clouds with her laughing as we drifted over Harper, the people below shrinking. But then Papa said it couldn't be done.

It's not that I don't trust Mama. In fact, I'd follow her to the moon if she could show me the way. The trouble is, Mama doesn't always know where she's going. She's like a feather floating in the wind and Papa, he's the man who holds her to earth and makes sure that she doesn't float away forever. I guess Papa must have let go for a minute or two sometime back, so Mama was drifting off without me. I hated Papa for letting her go.

Marie Fontaine's School of Dance

THINGS WERE GETTING OUT OF CONTROL. I WANTED PAPA TO stay faithful to Mama. I wanted him to go out and find her and bring her home. I wanted her to decide that she couldn't be without us anymore and arrive on the doorstep, battered suitcase in her hand, hat clenched over the handle, eyes red and blurry with tears. She'd beg us to forgive her. I'd run to her, hugging her, kissing her until she laughed. Papa would be there too. He'd stare down at Mama in relieved anger.

He'd be glad to know she was all right, but mad at her for leaving. That was the whole problem. I was beginning to realize that Papa didn't want Mama back. If he did, he wouldn't be flirting with Miss Ross, helping her out of her car, inviting her to our house to see Mama's garden. That was powerful flirting—adultery in fact.

Thanks to Mrs. Owens, I knew just what adultery meant. Unsatisfied with the wife-stealing explanation, I had to know just exactly what adultery was; so the Monday after Miss Ross came to our house, I raised my hand in religion class. Mrs. Owens was talking about the sin of coveting your neighbor's house. Since she was talking about coveting again, I thought it was the perfect time to bring up adultery. I waited until she was standing right next to me, then stood up with my hand in the air.

She near about jumped onto my desk, I'd startled her so. "Land's sake, girl, sit down." I took my seat. Mrs. Owens adjusted her bifocals, then asked, "What is it, Nissa?"

"Mrs. Owens, does adultery mean baby making with a person you're not married to?"

I felt a sharp sting in my face before I realized she'd slapped me. "I won't have you using such language in the house of God."

"Yes, ma'am." I bowed my head, hoping she'd still answer the question.

Luckily, she did. She pulled on the hem of her blouse to straighten the wrinkles, then said, "Now, to answer your question. Adultery is having any romantic thoughts about a person who isn't your spouse or doing any romantic things with a person you aren't married to."

So, Papa was committing adultery with Miss Ross and I learned just how serious he was about his sin when I caught him snipping columbines in the garden. I'd already brought in a nice bouquet for Mama's room, so I knew they had to be for someone else. I asked him who they were for, and he sniffed a blossom saying, "Miss Ross. Aren't you supposed to be getting ready for school, Neesay?"

"Aren't you supposed to be married to Mama?" I said, hoping he'd finally feel guilty for all his adultery. Mama says you always remember your sins if you have someone like a preacher there to remind you.

"What makes you say such a thing?"

"Because you're married to Mama, but you're giving Mama's flowers to Miss Ross."

He went inside. I thought he was so ashamed he'd gone to his room. Made me feel kind of guilty myself, but he came back without the flowers and told me to sit down on the back steps.

"Nissa," he said, pulling at the braid on my shoulder. Mama said that was his way of saying "I love you" while he's talking about something else. He said, "I know by what you've heard over at the post office that you think your mama left town with another man."

"Yeah." I couldn't deny it. Papa knew that everyone in town talked about it as if I didn't know what they meant. Grown-ups can be so dumb.

"Well, whether or not she's with another man, by leaving, Mama's saying she doesn't want to be my wife anymore. So, even though it makes me sad to be without your mama, I need to find a new wife."

"Does that mean I have to find a new mama if my real mama has another baby?"

"You didn't lose your mama, Nissa. You'll always be your mama's daughter. Nothing's going to change that, but your mama can't be a day-to-day mother for you anymore. That's why I need to find a new wife, so you can have a day-to-day mama."

"I don't want Miss Ross as any kind of mama." I stood up to let him know I was steaming mad and ready to walk to Buffalo. That's what Mama says gets a man's attention. You get so mad you're ready to walk off to the coldest place on earth just to cool down. I've been to Buffalo. They have ice there that forms on the eaves of the houses and doesn't melt for weeks.

Papa put his hands on my shoulders. He didn't even have to get up because I'm kind of short and Papa's tall enough to reach the lowest branch in the oak tree in the front yard. Mama threw his hat into the tree one day because she wanted him to take us to Gainesburg for the Parish Fair instead of going to work.

"Nissa, you don't know Miss Ross. That's why I want the three of us to go on a picnic. You two can get to know each other. I think she'll make you a fine mama."

I thought about it for a while and started to sink. If Papa was ready to marry another woman, that meant that there was no way my mama was ever coming back.

"I have to go to school!" I shouted to Papa, as I ran out the back gate. I wanted to be as far away from him as possible. He'd given up on Mama. She'd left with another man and he'd let her go. It was his fault. He should have given her the things she'd wanted. I'd done all I could. I was the one who brought her back the first time. It was his turn, his responsibility.

I made it to the bus stop on the corner of Jefferson and Maxwell, but I was crying so much I couldn't catch my breath. I stood there hugging the bus sign, praying I could just disappear. I thought maybe I could sneak on the bus and travel down to New Orleans, find myself the biggest, sturdiest steamboat, and float off the end of the world. Sliding down to the ground, I could remember Mama sitting by that sign on her steamer trunk.

It had been my first day of school and Mama had walked me there. I carried my shoes in my hand as we walked through Gideon Kelly's field to the wooden schoolhouse sitting in a grove of bald cypress by Sutton's Creek.

"You can put your feet in the creek during recess if you get hot during class," Mama told me as she squeezed my hand.

"And feed the fishes dough balls."

Mama laughed. "Some days I regret telling you what I used to do with my school lunch."

"I like feeding the fishes."

Mama scooped me up. "I like you!" I laughed, but she looked sad. "I'm going to miss you, Nissa." She hugged me so tight it hurt.

"I'll run home from school, Mama."

She backed away waving. "Have fun!"

"I will!" I yelled back.

I ran to school because I was afraid I wouldn't see Mama if I looked over my shoulder. As the youngest student, I had to sit in the front row. I was staring straight into Mrs. Collier's belly when I looked up from the primer she gave me. I was always looking up to clear my mind of the thought that Mama wouldn't be at home when I got there.

By recess, I couldn't take it anymore. I ran down the school steps, then straight home. Her room was barer than Mr. Minkie's store before a hurricane. There wasn't a single thing left in it that could be carried away in one hand.

I went out to the garden to find her, but the garden was empty. I mean empty. Mama'd pulled up every living flower, dumped them all in a big old pile, then burned them. The burnt roses smelled so sweet it was hard to breathe. I saw footsteps in the hibiscus bed. Mama must have walked through the hibiscus to get to the gate. There, there was another set of footprints. They were bigger than my two feet end to end. They were definitely a man's footprints, but not Papa's, because his feet weren't that big. I suppose she'd had a man carry her steamer trunk. At the time, as a child of five, I was sure she'd gone off with some man. I knew less about adultery back then, so I figured they'd just gone off together as friends.

I'd run out to the alley calling for her, but she wasn't there; just her muddy footprints which led out to the curb. I ran to the street. Looking both ways, I saw nobody but old Mr. Trenton who was watching for burglars from the duck blind in his backyard. He was robbed while hunting one year, so he went burglar hunting every time duck season came around.

I was crying by the time I reached the corner. I could cry at the drop of a feather when I was five. I would probably have stood there and bawled until Papa came to find me if I hadn't caught sight of Mama. She was sitting at the corner of Jefferson and Maxwell, perched on her steamer trunk right below the sign for the bus. I wondered if she was waiting for the bus that came through on Monday nights and got you to New Orleans before breakfast on Tuesday.

"Mama!" I screamed, as I ran to her. She looked so rigid and small sitting on that box in a long black dress and a wide-brim hat that hid her face.

She didn't even look at me. She shifted to the side and showed her back to me. "Go home, Nissa."

"But Mama," I said, coming around to stand in front of her. Her hat was pushed down over her eyes and her chin looked as pointed as a beak. "What are you doing here?"

"I'm going to learn to dance professionally."

"Where?"

"Marie Fontaine's School of Dance on La Rue de La Rouge, New Orleans."

"You're going to New Orleans without me and Papa?" The thought of having to be without my mama was unbearable. I was instantly in tears.

"I can learn to dance before you finish school for the year." Mama looked at her knees as she spoke. "I'll be back then. In the meantime, you and Papa can replant my garden and spend all your time together."

"I want to be with you." I sunk down onto the cement wheel that was holding up the bus sign.

"Nissa, I can't spend hours in an empty house with nothing to do. I just can't do it."

"But I need you, Mama." I jumped up to hug her, but she spun to the other side of the trunk.

"Your papa can take care of you."

I crawled up on the trunk to hug her arm. I desperately needed to show her how much she was hurting me and make her understand why she couldn't leave. "I'll get all cold inside without you."

"Cold inside?" Mama looked right at me and it tickled my insides.

"You keep me warm, Mama." I snuggled up to her and she put her arm around me.

"How about we both go to New Orleans?"

"Then Papa would get cold."

"We wouldn't want that." Mama gave me a squeeze.

I jumped down off the trunk, then tugged on her arm to get her to follow me. "Let's go home."

"Not yet." Mama pulled her hand out of mine, then patted the trunk, gesturing for me to sit down. I climbed up as she held up a cardboard box the size of her jewelry box, tied shut with string. "Let's give the dinner I packed to the bus driver."

"Why?"

"There's bound to be someone on the bus without the money for cafe food."

"Oh." I nodded. "That's nice."

Mama shrugged. "I won't eat it."

The bus came around the corner. It was as big as the train cars I saw crossing Main Street three times a week. I couldn't understand how something that big could stay up while going around corners without rails to hold it in place. The bus hissed to a halt in front of us.

When the door opened, Mama handed me the box, then lowered me to the ground. I ran up the steps. "Give this to someone without money," I said, handing the box to the driver. "In case they get hungry."

"Thanks." The driver smiled and I saw that he had one gold tooth. I was thinking of pirates when he looked over my shoulder and shouted to Mama, "Hey lady, you getting on?"

"No." Mama stood up and held out her hand. "Nissa."

I ran back to the trunk to take her hand and we walked off. The driver cursed as he slammed the door, then drove off with his bus grinding and growling. We walked home, leaving the trunk alone on the curb.

When we got home, we sat in the garden. Mama threw her ankle boots at the back steps and sat down on the flagstones. Pulling the dress down over her knees, she hugged her legs and started to cry. Mama was always silent when she cried. I mean, she didn't sob, she just let the tears roll down her face.

I wanted to touch her, to kiss away the tears, but I knew she had something to tell me. Mama never cried in front of me unless she had something real important to say. "I didn't really mean to leave you, Nissa."

She reached over to pull me close. "You're the best thing God ever gave me." I felt so safe and warm there next to her with her arm over my shoulder. She cleared her throat, then said, "I'm such a fool. I thought threatening to leave would make your father come running after me. I didn't want to hurt you. I just wanted your father to miss me. To need me."

I whispered, "Papa loves you."

"Yes, yes he does." Her hands were shaking as she looked at her wedding ring. We sat in silence for a moment staring at the ground; there was nothing but piles of drying flowers left. Papa would have to go all the way back to Chicago to buy more bare roots to restart the rosebushes. "Look at this mess."

"We can plant again."

"Nissa." She shook me as she smiled. "The eternal optimist."

Mama was silent for a moment as she drew circles in the ash on a flagstone. Clearing her throat, she said, "The doctor told me to start over. When you lose something dear to you, you start over."

"What did you lose, Mama?"

"Nothing." She hugged me. "We better get cooking. A good meal will keep your papa out of this garden for a while."

I still wanted to know what Mama lost, but I was sure asking her again would make her cry and I didn't want that, so I went where Mama led me. I said, "He'll be mad."

"That's right." Mama stood up, then turned to take my hand. "What do you say? Shall we make muffins in the shape of tiny men?"

"Just like Grandma Neesay!" I shouted.

"Just like her," Mama whispered.

That evening, Papa came home just as Mama was putting supper on the table. He picked up a hot, man-shaped blueberry muffin and tossed it back and forth between his hands as he said, "How was the first day of school, Neesay?"

"Fine."

"Just fine?" he asked, biting the head off his muffin. He stepped over to Mama and gave her a kiss on the neck, saying, "Thanks for the muffin."

Mama put her fingers over the spot where he kissed her as if she wanted to keep it safe.

I told Papa, "I didn't learn anything new. I'd rather stay here with Mama."

"Well," Papa looked at Mama with a smile on his face, but she didn't smile back. "What is it? Don't tell me you don't want her to go to school either?"

Mama was rinsing out the skillet. "Why does she need it? Thanks to you, she can already read. I taught her colors and numbers. She doesn't need to start school now."

Papa turned to face the sink. "And next year, after you've taught her how to add and subtract, you'll tell me she doesn't need to go until the year after that."

I hated it when they turned their backs on me and talked as if I wasn't there. I smashed my muffin man flat on my plate as Mama said, "Is there anything wrong with home schooling?"

"You didn't finish high school, Heirah. Do you want that for your daughter?"

Mama raised her hand to flick water in Papa's face. "Are you saying I'm stupid, Ivar?"

"No, I'm saying a high school diploma's the fastest ticket to college."

"She's five!" Mama pointed at me. "Five years old and you're sending her off to college! You just can't wait to take my child away from me, can you?"

Mama turned to stare at Papa. He didn't even open his mouth. She threw the dishrag at him, then rushed out of the room. I heard her running up the steps and knew I wouldn't see her for the rest of the night. She'd lock her door and stay in her room until dawn. She always did that when she was mad.

Papa didn't say anything. He just threw the rag back into the sink, sat down, then started to eat his supper. When he saw I wasn't eating, he pointed his fork at my plate. "Eat up, Neesay."

"What did Mama lose?"

"What?"

"Mama said the doctor told her to start over if you lose something dear to you. What did she lose?"

Papa turned sideways in his chair. "Why do you ask that?"

I was embarrassed. I felt like a tattletale, but I knew Papa would explain things. "Mama pulled up the garden and packed her trunk to leave, then came back and said the doctor told her to start over."

"Slow down, Nissa. Tell me about the trunk. Was Mama leaving?"

"I came home and Mama was on the curb waiting for the bus that goes to New Orleans."

"Today?"

"Right before we made supper."

Papa looked up at the ceiling, then down at me. "But you stopped her."

"I told her we'd get cold without her."

"Did you." Papa gripped his napkin with a fist. I hoped I hadn't made him mad.

"What did she lose, Papa?"

He looked at me and forced a smile. "I don't know. Maybe she thought she'd lost you. With you off at school all day, maybe she felt alone."

"She said she couldn't be alone and she wanted you to run after her."

Papa wiped his face with his hand. "Nissa, Nissa." He patted his lap. I climbed into it. "We're making you grow old before your time."

"What?"

"Your crazy parents with all their yelling and running away are making you grow up too fast."

"I'm only five."

"Not in here." He poked me gently in the heart, then held me close.

"Papa?"

"Yes."

"Will you tell Mama she'll never lose me?"

"I will."

Papa didn't say anything else. I wanted him to talk to me, to tell me everything would be okay. To tell me I could spend my days with Mama so she didn't feel lonely. Then she'd never leave us.

Papa took me over to the Carrolls'. He sent me and Mary to her room, then talked to Mr. and Mrs. Carroll on the porch. I don't know what they said, but I wasn't about to stay there when I knew something important was about to happen at my house. Mary and I snuck out her window, then down the alley, and into our garden. The only problem was we didn't have anywhere to hide at my house. With all the plants cut down, there was nothing to hide behind in the garden.

"Let's go up there," Mary suggested, pointing at the trellis going up the kitchen wall. It went all the way up to the roof over the sink and we could crawl into my window from there.

"Okay."

On the way up, I slipped. Mary had her hand on my back, so I didn't fall. It took a lot of effort to swing ourselves onto the roof, but my window was open, so we got inside pretty easily.

Crouched next to the wall my room shared with Mama's room, we listened. I expected to hear them arguing, but I heard music. It was the radio. I could hear the crackling snaps it always made. Papa had carried it upstairs. It was as big as a piano bench and a billion times heavier, but Papa had carried it to Mama's room. I could hear their feet shuffling across the floor.

"What are they doing?" Mary asked.

"Dancing," I told her. "I think they're dancing."

They spoke in whispers, so we couldn't hear a word, but it was wonderful to hear the murmur of a waltz with the shuffle, slide, shuffle of their feet. Papa was showing Mama just how much he loved her.

I was ready to burst, I was so happy, but Mary was nervous. She didn't want her parents to find out that we'd snuck back into my house, so we hurried back to her house. We went undetected. I slept on Mary's floor that night and Mrs. Carroll sent me home for breakfast.

When I came home, I expected to spend the day with Mama. When she saw me come in, Mama kissed me on top of the head, then took my hand to lead me upstairs. "Let's go get you dressed."

"For school?"

"Yes, for school."

Mama'd had a night of romance, but had lost the fight to keep me at home. I had to go to school. And making me go to school wasn't Papa's last word on Mama's plan to leave us. When I got home that afternoon, Mama's steamer trunk was sitting in the middle of the hallway. Papa had stripped it down to the metal, then repainted it blue. His favorite color's blue. Mama likes purple. He did paint red flowers on it though. I guess that meant he was mad at her for leaving, but glad she'd decided to stay.

* * *

Still, he never helped Mama replant the garden. I did. We worked on it every night before I went to bed. I had to take a bath every night to get rid of the smell of humus and to soften up the gook beneath my nails. When I lay in bed at night, it felt like my arms were still digging. In my dreams, I was kneeling down in the rose bed, scooping out dirt and flinging it over my shoulder, hoping each time I went back for more dirt that I'd uncover a secret tunnel that led all the way to China. Mama and I could harvest the bright red poppies that grow in China and bring them home to plant in our garden.

It was great to be in the garden with Mama. It gave us a chance to talk. I thought she didn't love Papa and me anymore, but she set me straight. We were replanting the hibiscus bed. Mama was kneading the soil to break up all the clumps. She had her back to the house, so she didn't see Papa standing at his bedroom window, looking down at us. He wasn't smiling. He wasn't frowning. He was just looking. That empty expression made me ask, "Do you love Papa?"

Mama tossed some dirt into the air. "You've got the mind of an ageless woman, Nissa."

"What?" I giggled.

"Asking me about love." She smudged my cheek with dirt. "Little children don't ask questions like that."

"I did."

"All right then." She nodded. Pressing her hands together, she said, "My Grandfather Tipton used to say that to see love clearly, you've got to squint your eyes,"—Mama squinted and I laughed—"pucker your heart,"—Mama didn't move, but I believed she was making her heart pucker—"and blow." She blew dirt into my hair.

Wiping the dirt out, I asked, "What's that mean?"

"It means love is darn tough to pin down. You can't really see it or touch it. Or describe for that matter. It's a risky affair. You fall in love, but inside your heart, there are these feuding brothers who can't stop fighting over some dumb thing like who gets the biggest piece of rhubarb pie. You can never quite get control of it. When there's a truce, love's the finest thing a soul can hold except the peace of God, but there's always a new battle."

What she said made no sense. I remember it, but I still don't understand it. All I wanted to know was if she loved Papa or not. "Do you love Papa?"

She smiled, "Let's just say the McGuire brothers are happy to be together, but there's a little grumbling going on."

We finished the hibiscus bed that night and I went to bed wondering what she meant by all that talk of love. I fell asleep thinking I had feuding brothers inside my heart. Mama used that story whenever she and Papa were fighting. If I came home and Papa was in the den with the door closed and Mama caught me wondering why it wasn't open to let the breeze blow through, she'd say, "The McGuire brothers are feuding again."

I wasn't too fond of those McGuire brothers. I wished they'd just bury their differences. And Mama still hadn't really answered my question about whether she loved Papa or not. I guess our little talk didn't help me much. All of

Mama's talk about love just confused me. Love was kites. Love was fighting brothers. I'd never see it clearly no matter what I did. All I knew back then was that it was enough to keep us together as a family.

Of course I was wrong and I guess Mama knew it, too. After her first attempt to leave, Mama started going to painting classes at Mrs. Bovisch's. She said she was happy waiting for me to come home because she could paint while I was away. She painted a whole garden on my bedroom wall. There was a large rock in the center of the mural where I imagined myself sitting and looking at the curry-yellow lilies Mama had painted above my dresser. I could even dangle my feet in the monkey grass around the rock. When I closed my eyes, I could almost smell the ruby-dot hibiscus along the floorboards beside my dresser. They made me thirsty for tea. What I wanted most was to be able to climb the ivy that scaled my wall and sit on the roof over our house and look at the stars.

Butterflies and Norway

PART OF ME KNEW MAMA WASN'T GOING TO STAY. MAMA never gives up on an idea. I told myself she'd stay if I were always there to be with her. But when I saw a suitcase sitting in the hallway one morning, my blood filled with ice. I was sure she was leaving. I realized I'd secretly been waiting for her to decide she'd leave. I never let myself think it was going to happen, but somewhere deep down, I knew it would. Mama was only cleaning the closet that day, but the truth was she'd only been biding her time.

Harper just wasn't big enough for Mama. She'd tried to make it grow with the murals—from the painted garden path that led out of our kitchen to the shelves full of books with leather covers and gold lettering on the wall of Papa's study. Mama made our house grander and more magical than any Harper had ever seen. She seemed to be happy there, painting a new mural, tending her flowers, or playing with me. And then the Sawdust Man came along to ruin it all. I was a fool to think she'd stay.

I'd done all I could to make Harper better for her. When I wasn't at school or playing jacks with Mary, I was with Mama in the garden or playacting with her upstairs. We had wonderful times together. We'd laugh until it sounded like we had one voice. I felt so small when I thought about Mama leaving all that behind. Wasn't she as happy as I was when we did things like make little people and horses out of cookie dough? Wasn't she the one who said she'd never had so much fun in her life when we slid down the hill behind the church on the huge baking pans they had for the bake-off?

I couldn't let it be my fault that Mama left. I'd done everything I could, so it must have been Papa's fault. When did he go sliding down a hill with Mama? He spent a lot of time in the study poking his nose in books. If he wasn't there, he was over at the newspaper office getting all inky and sweaty. Last thing I remember him doing with Mama was building a little wishing well in the garden. He'd brought home a pile of bricks the summer before she left and suggested the idea to Mama. She was so excited, she ran right out to the car and made a bag out of her skirt to start hauling bricks out to the garden. They worked all afternoon in silence—pointing to what they wanted. Mama and Papa were silent partners. It was like they knew each other's thoughts—passing the butter without being asked, bringing a sweater or a blanket from another room when the other was cold. They were meant to be together, but Mama had left with another man.

Papa didn't spend enough time with Mama. He let her forget how much he loved her. He forgot to say how he felt quite often. I couldn't remember the last time he told me he loved me. It was Papa's fault that Mama was gone and he was already looking for a new wife. I hoped God would zap him with lightning. He needed a good jolt to wake him up to what he did, then maybe he'd go after Mama. If he told her how much he loved her and promised to be with her every day, then maybe, just maybe Mama would come home.

Papa didn't agree. He said Mama didn't want him as a husband anymore, so he was hunting for another wife. He'd picked Miss Ross and he wanted me to agree with his choice. I didn't, but there was nothing I could do. He wanted the three of us to go on a picnic. It was silly to waste such a beautiful Saturday by spending it with Miss Ross. But regardless of what I wanted, Papa was going to finish at Mr. Minkie's, then come pick me up so we could go get Miss Ross and find the perfect spot for a picnic. The perfect spot for Miss Ross was at the bottom of a lake.

I didn't want to go on a picnic with the glove woman, but I figured I'd better, or she'd have my papa lying in the grass on a picnic cloth or even locking lips like April Carroll does with Fenton Journiette when they go on picnics after church. I bet it's a sin to kiss on Sundays, but April probably doesn't mind sinning. April's an accomplished sinner and she's got seven engagement rings in her jewelry box to prove it. Mama says you don't notice sins as much after they start piling up a bit.

I figured Papa had gotten used to adultery. He probably didn't notice when he was being too sweet on Miss Ross. They hadn't made any babies yet, but that's not the only thing adulterers do.

* * *

Waiting for Papa, I sat curled up in Mama's window, hugging the pillow she slept on. It smelled like her. That vinegary sweet smell was one sweetness shy of rose petals. Thinking back on her leaving with the Sawdust Man, I guessed I wasn't enough anymore. I felt like my insides were filled with lead.

Just then, Papa came clomping up the stairs. I knew he was coming to take me on the stupid picnic with Miss Ross. "Ready to go chase butterflies, Neesay?" he asked, as he leaned into the room.

I moaned, then said, "Carry me, Papa." If Papa could get my dead weight to the car, I'd go on his silly picnic.

Papa scooted around Mama's bed, then bent down by the window. "You sick, Nissa?"

I didn't want to make Papa sad, so I said, "No, Papa, I'm just tired."

"All right." Papa slipped his arms under me and stood up without so much as taking a breath. It felt as if I were floating as he carried me outside. I wondered if baby birds felt that way when they were snuggled up in their nest on a sapling branch and a soft wind began to blow.

"Want me to get you a blanket?" Papa asked, as he set me down in the backseat of Betsy, our old car.

"No, Papa, I'm fine." Papa was being real good to me, but I didn't want Mama—wherever she was—to think I was running off to be with a new mama. I figured I'd pretend to fall asleep right off, so Miss Ross wouldn't blather at me when she got in the car. She was the last person I wanted to make happy.

As we drove off toward Miss Ross's house in the country,

I daydreamed about the picnics we used to have. We had two picnic traditions—bird watching and butterfly chasing. Before eating, we layed out on the grass and stared at the sky, watching the birds fly overhead, then told stories about the places they were traveling to. Papa always said the blue jays were flying into the sky for another coat of blue on their feathers. Mama took it seriously and told us where the birds were going, right down to the color of the mailbox at the house where the bird ate its meals.

After dinner, Mama and I liked to chase butterflies. As soon as Mama had her last bite of lunch, we'd shuck our shoes off, then take hands to go butterfly hunting. Mama usually saw one first; she'd creep forward on the balls of her feet, her hands cupped to hold the butterfly without hurting it. When the insect took flight, Mama squealed in joy, then ran with it, jumping into the air with long leaps. I can swear to the fact that I've seen my mother soar right over Sutton's Creek in pursuit of a great purple hairstreak. The purple-winged butterfly drifted over the water in a jagged little flight that made it seem like two of Mama's rose petals flapping their way over a creek. Mama leapt off the shore and for a split second, as she went over the water rushing around slick rocks, I was sure she could hold herself there forever, or fly away after that tiny bug and disappear into the clouds. Of course she came down hard on the other side, nearly crumbling to her knees before she regained her balance and continued her pursuit.

Mama never really caught butterflies, she just chased them. She said it made the food we ate get digested faster so we could take naps without having bad dreams when we got home. It worked, too. When I took a nap, I always dreamed of becoming a butterfly and flying up in the heavens with Mama.

Mama was magic and fire. She could be dancing with a flow and bounce that made me think she could fly, then she was eating some part of me that would never grow back. Just like the plants in our garden, Mama had burned me by leaving. She made me mad and angry at a woman I didn't even know. Miss Ross and I had to pay for Mama's wild ways. From one day to the next, I could never count on knowing whether Mama was magic or fire.

Slouched in the backseat, I thought how nice it would be if Mama was magic all the time. Miss Ross pulled me right out of a daydream where I was chasing a monarch when she climbed into the car saying, "Morning, Mr. Bergen."

"Good morning, Miss Ross."

"My, Nissa looks all roses and milk curled up in the back like that."

I was ready to pop up and shout, "The Lord knows when you lie and so do I." Of course she didn't lie so much as sound like she was selling me to my own father, as if I were some product sold over the radio.

I heard Papa chuckle with his coffeepot-bubble laugh. "She sure is."

"We have a fine day for a picnic," Miss Ross said, and I had to admit she sounded a bit like she was singing.

"Indeed," Papa replied.

They were quiet for a while, then Miss Ross kind of

shouted, "Have you heard from Heirah Rae?" I was mad that she used Mama's calling name, but I was real eager to hear if Papa might say yes.

"No," Papa said, short and deep. She'd made him sad, but I was glad to know Papa was still missing Mama.

Miss Ross sat up in the front seat as stiff as a wrought-iron gate, saying, "I hope you believe me when I tell you that I'm praying she's well."

"Me, too." I wanted to pipe up and agree with Papa, but I enjoyed listening to them from the backseat. I felt as if I were a bird hiding in a treetop, spying on the people riding in a swing which hung from the branches below me.

They didn't talk for a bit, then Miss Ross said, "I read your article about Norway this week. I love the way you describe things so true and clear. It makes me think I could be standing in Oslo myself."

"Thank you." Papa chuckled. He was embarrassed.

"How old were you when you came to the United States?"

"Only five."

"You have a fantastic memory to recall so much."

"I get a lot of the details from the letters I receive from my family back in Norway."

Miss Ross shivered.

"Are you all right?" Papa asked.

"Oh yes," she laughed. "I was just imagining what it must be like cutting chunks out of a frozen lake to drag home to an icehouse. Brr!" She rubbed her arms.

The thought of Norway made me chilly. The only thing I liked to hear about Norway was about the ocean shore at

Bergen where Papa's grandparents had lived. Papa even said the city was named after our ancestors. He said that in certain places the shore was jagged like the teeth of shark and the water was so churned up by the winds that it rose up in frothy white tufts like egg whites when they're beaten into peaks. I could imagine myself tossing and twisting in a sturdy little boat on those wild waters, but in my Norway there was no cold and the snow was warm and soft to the touch.

I hated the cold. Papa loved it. When we went to Buffalo, New York, so Papa could buy a printing press from a man who was selling his newspaper, Mama and I stayed in the hotel. Not Papa. From the window we could see him running and jumping in the snow. He even got a few local kids to help him build a snowman. All bundled up in their coats, scarves, mittens, and hats, those kids looked like they were about to suffocate in all those clothes. But the snowman looked so real the way Papa carved out his arms, his legs, and even the slope of his neck.

That man of snow was so much better than any I'd ever seen in a storybook that I'd had to go up to the window to have a closer look. Papa had stood back and clapped his hands together to dust the snow off his gloves. The snow looked like sawdust spinning away from a saw blade the way it flew up in the air. Papa looked up to our window. Seeing me, he'd waved. Part of me had wanted to go down there and help Papa build a little snow daughter for that snowman, but most of me was too afraid of the cold to even think of stepping outside in that air that could freeze my breath into ice on my scarf.

* * *

Thinking back about that cold winter in 1932, when I was ten, made me rub my back against the seat of the car to warm up. Just the memory of Buffalo made me cold. Miss Ross was still blabbering away about Norway.

"It seems like such a romantic place," she said, pulling her straw hat down to shield her eyes from the sun. "Do you ever dream of returning?"

"Every time I smell old fish."

I had to stuff my skirt into my mouth to keep from laughing. Miss Ross was too dumb to know he'd made a joke. Papa just let it pass, but I knew Miss Ross wasn't doing well with Papa. Mama would have been smart enough to laugh at Papa's "old fish" joke. She knew his family ate the fish his uncles couldn't sell. She wouldn't go around flattering Papa to make him like her. She'd let her true self shine, bare feet and all.

Papa looked back at me to see how I was doing. I clamped my eyes shut, so he'd believe I was still sleeping and tell Miss Ross what he was really thinking. I guess he turned back to face the road because Miss Ross piped up all of a sudden, saying, "Ivar, may I call you Ivar?"

Papa said, "Certainly."

April Carroll says using a man's calling name means a woman wants to kiss him, and if he doesn't tell the woman to call him by his family name, he wants to kiss her, too. I was getting a little worried that Miss Ross might've been getting ready to kiss Papa. Flirting was one thing, but kissing led to baby making and that was too much. I took a peek and saw that she was looking right at Papa, smiling. I turned and, sure enough, Papa was smiling back. I jumped up screaming, "Watch the road!"

Papa jumped and made the car skid toward the edge of the road. I was knocked back into the seat and Miss Ross screamed as if I'd just slammed her toe in the door. I wish I had crushed her toe, then maybe she wouldn't try so hard to get close to Papa.

"Nissa," Papa barked, once he got the car going straight. "Why'd you scream?"

"You weren't watching the road." I scooted up so I could rest my arms on the back of Papa's seat and force Miss Ross to keep her distance.

"You don't yell at the driver, Nissa. That's dangerous," Papa said with a big sigh.

I wanted to tell him it wasn't dangerous to yell at people who were about to commit adultery. It was a good thing in fact. God was happy with me, I'm sure.

Picnic

PAPA PICKED THE WRONG SPOT FOR OUR PICNIC. HE DIDN'T PICK a fallow cotton field dotted with the stiff brown stems of old plants, where the ground is covered with mounds of dirt stubbled with grass. Although the mounds would keep me stumbling, there was room to chase butterflies and watch the birds fly. Instead of a fallow field, Papa chose a cramped old island on the Amite River. With the weeping willows yawning over us like the tangled hair of an old woman, I couldn't even see much of the sky. With our wool blanket laid out on the prickly grass, we took up most of the island that wasn't covered with trees. I couldn't even see the other bank of the river through the dense woods beyond our picnic sight. I'd get lost chasing after butterflies in those twisted old cypress trees.

Mama would have hated the island with its weeping willows and closed-in prickly grass space. Mama liked to spread our blanket in an open field filled with wildflowers. On the island, we'd be hard-pressed to see the birds flying overhead with all the trees in our way.

As we sat down to set up our picnic, I dreamed about a

picnic we'd had a few years ago. It was the Fourth of July. We'd gone out to the field just below Sutton's Creek. Mama'd had on her pretty blue dress with the rose-shaped buttons.

An indigo bunting flew overhead, showing off his bright blue feathers and stretching his black wings into the wind. "He's going north to get out of this heat," Mama said, licking the sweat from her upper lip.

Papa leaned back to rest his head on Mama's belly. "You believe so?"

"Probably going all the way to Minnesota. If we could catch him now, we could send a message to Knut." Mama arched her back, then barked out Grandpa's name as if she were howling at the sun: "Knut!"

Papa laughed. "Papa would probably trap it for its color."

"What do you mean?" I asked.

"He loves bright colors so much he'd want to keep the bird with him, so he'd put it in a cage."

"Fifty odd years of Norwegian winters can do that to a person," Mama whispered.

I said, "I'm glad we don't have winter here in Louisiana."

"That's because you've never played in the snow," Papa told me.

"But it's cold and it'll freeze you," I said.

Mama giggled and made Papa's head bob on her tummy. She raised her hands in the air and lowered her voice to say, "Yes, but there are castles in that frozen rain. It's better than the beach. Snow holds together better than sand. Just think of the things you could build."

"I can tell you've never tried to make a snowman," Papa said. Perhaps he didn't believe in Mama's castle, but I wanted to be there in Mama's snow kingdom, to walk inside those castles of ice where I could see my breath create puffs of icy smoke. In my dreams, the snow and ice was cool to the touch, but not cold enough to frost your skin. The wintry world I dreamt of would be far better than sitting on an island surrounded by gangly willows. I was sweating so bad I could feel it trickle down my back.

I could almost feel the snow against my skin when Miss Ross interrupted my dream with another one of her stupid questions. "What are you thinking about?" she asked, taking the food out of the basket as Papa flattened the edges of our blanket.

"Ice," I told her. "I'm thinking of castles of ice."

She shook her head and laughed. "You think of the strangest things."

Papa said, "She takes after her mother."

Strangest things? I wanted to scream. Besides, being like Mama was a good thing. I wouldn't be a boring, glove-wearing, flirty old maid. I'd be a magical, free gardener with a family who loved me.

I was ready to come out spitting and biting; then Papa shook his head and smiled, saying, "Heirah can make the simplest thing seem important. She once had me staring at a piece of lint to see how it resembled the hand of a child."

I was glad Papa was still talking about Mama. She'd been gone for six months, but he was still talking about her as if she were away for the weekend. Miss Ross blushed and bowed her head. She knew my mama had left a lot of herself behind. Papa and I were keeping Mama right there between us. In our minds, she was sitting there shoeless with heat-curled brown hair and a purple rose held between her fingers. I smiled.

Sitting on her knees, Miss Ross hopped up a little as if she were trying to fly, saying, "Heirah was always so imaginative, so, so alive." Papa hummed in agreement, then Miss Ross added, "I always wished I'd had the courage to talk to her. Be her friend."

"Courage?" Papa asked the question. I wanted to know the answer.

Miss Ross laughed. "I know it's silly, but Heirah seemed so distant, unapproachable even."

"Why?" Papa asked.

"I don't know. I guess I always figured she'd laugh at me."

Mama would have. She'd know Miss Ross was a phony. Mama would figure she had warts under those pretty gloves. Papa sighed. "Probably so."

"Did she laugh at you?" Miss Ross asked Papa.

"A lot," Papa laughed.

I was getting sick of hearing them jabber as Miss Ross sat there with a plate of cold chicken wings, jellied cranberries, and cornbread in her hand. I shouted, "She never laughed at me, so, can we eat?"

"Heavens, I forgot." She handed me the plate. "I wasn't trying to starve you, Nissa."

"No?" I said, biting into my cornbread.

"Nissa!" Papa stared at me, his face taut. Miss Ross folded her hands in her lap. Her lips quivered as if she wanted to say something, then she just took up her plate. Papa stood up. "I forgot the wine," he said, walking off without looking back.

"He's leaving so we can talk," I said, letting the corn-bread crumbs fall out of my mouth.

"You're a clever person, Nissa," Miss Ross said, cutting her cornbread into four squares. "And quite selfish, too."

"Why do you say that?"

"Because you want things your way and your way only. You get that from your mother, too." She looked up at me. Her long, thin nose and tight, red lips made her look like the face on Mama's talcum-powder box—forceful, mysterious, even a bit pretty. I imagined that lady running a news-paper as a real job and needing talcum powder to soak up real sweat.

"What do you know about my mama?"

"I respected your mother for her ability to say exactly how she felt no matter who she was talking to, but some-times she could've just said nothing. I mean, I've seen her waltz right up to Mrs. Dayton before church and tell her an inch of her slip was showing."

"What's wrong with that?"

"It's rude, Nissa."

"It's the truth."

"All right." Miss Ross put her plate down, then moved over to sit straight in front of me. "Nissa, your hair's a mess. Did you even comb it this morning?"

I ran my fingers through my hair. It was snarly. "So?"

"Your dress looks like you ran it over a cheese grater." She pulled at the hem of my dress. It had a few moth holes in it, but it was my favorite. Mama had given it to me for my ninth birthday and, even though it was tight in the sleeves and a couple of inches too short, it was so comfortable I liked to sleep in it. What did it matter what I looked like? I was clean. I was comfortable. We were out in the middle of nowhere. Who was there to notice the holes in my dress and the snarls in my hair? I said, "So? It's better than sweating in a fancy dress and gloves."

"I suppose it doesn't matter if you don't care what people think about the way you look."

"I don't."

"Fine." Miss Ross held the cornbread between two fingers as if it were made out of glass. She ate one square in two bites. She was so careful, so particular, I had to hate her. We ate our cornbread in silence and I started praying Papa would get back soon so I didn't have to be alone with her any longer.

"Here's the wine," Papa said when he finally returned. He looked at me with a question in his eyes. Everything all right?

I wanted to tell him he'd picked the wrong woman to court. She was the exact opposite of everything Mama ever was. I couldn't understand why he'd even like a woman who was so prissy, unimaginative, and not the least bit magical. He walked past me, then sat down by Miss Ross, saying, "I can't wait to taste your cornbread, Lara."

I thought her cornbread tasted like sawdust. Sawdust. Did Mama like that dry, bitter taste? Is that what made her like the Sawdust Man? What made him better than my papa? Maybe he didn't say her name like a sigh when he was angry, as Papa did. I imagined it was even possible that the Sawdust Man liked eating rose petals in the rain or sitting on the roof on a sweltering summer night. If she had taken me with her when she left, would Mama have ever left me alone with the Sawdust Man? And would he have yelled at me for looking shabby? Maybe he'd have told me about the saws that could cut an entire tree in half, their deafening buzz, their jagged metal teeth. Perhaps he would have climbed one of those burly pine trees with spikes strapped to the bottom of his shoes. I wondered if he could climb all the way to the top of a tree and look down at me, so I looked as small as a bug. It was hard to imagine. Not because I couldn't picture those things. I just didn't want to admit the Sawdust Man could be a nice man like my papa.

As I thought about Mama and her Sawdust Man, I wondered if she was even thinking about me. She didn't even leave me a note. No good-bye. Her silly old Halloween card didn't make up for nothing.

I'd done my part that day. I'd given her a kiss when I'd left for school in the morning, but she didn't even tug my braid. She'd just turned around and gone inside the house. She'd probably started packing as soon as I walked out the front door. She'd taken the silver hairbrush she'd promised me and my favorite picture of Papa and me where we were all snuggled up together in the front seat of our old car, Betsy. She'd taken them both without even saying good-bye and left me with this witchy, sour woman. All so she could go off baby making with some strange man.

That was it. She hadn't taken me with her because I would be in the way. They couldn't do those flirty things in front of me. Damn. That's what good old Miss Ross had in mind, too. She was scooting up to my papa and pushing me away so she could make lovey with Papa.

Thinking about her trying to kiss my father made me so crazy mad, I jumped up and tossed my plate at Miss Ross. I turned just as she'd raised her hands to shield her face from flying chicken legs, then ran for the trees. I was going to jump into the water, swim to shore, then run home before Papa could stop me. I was all spit and fire, ready to burn up anything in my way. I was well into the water before I remembered I couldn't swim.

The greenish brown water began to swallow me with a rushing gurgle before I could scream. I fought hard to get to the surface, knowing Papa would be there to save me. I kicked and clawed, but no matter what I did, I only fought water. I was bound by water on all sides, with no air to relieve me. I had no strength. No motion. I was sure I was dying, just so my mama would be free to make more babies. The water tightened its grip on my waist and I melted into nothing.

Yellow Roses

NOTHING IS A HEAVY THING TO BE. YOUR MUSCLES DON'T work, so your body weighs more than your blood and bones. Your thoughts get too thin to put together. You can't do. You can't think. You're nothing.

The only thing harder than being nothing is trying to become something again. I suppose that's why Jesus was the only man who could come back from the dead after three days. Going from nothing to something had to be easy for God.

Me, I was burning hot with fever. I wanted to crawl out onto the porch to cool off. I took a deep breath to sit up in bed and it felt as if someone had lit a fire in my lungs.

Rubbing my chest, I tried to think of a way to stop the pain. My head felt as if it had been stuffed with cotton, making my thoughts all pudgy and edgeless. My mind was foggy, so I couldn't catch the beginning or the end of anything that crossed through my thoughts. Fish floated in water filled with cranberries and Mama's voice spoke to headless chickens with breading on their legs. I was sure I was going crazy, but I'd really drowned in the Amite River.

As Papa tells it, I'd thrashed around so much I got all

133

turned around. I was facing the riverbed not the surface of the water. My lungs filled up with water and I sank like a sack of kittens tied in with a rock, or so Dr. Swenson had told Papa when they let me out of the hospital. Poor Papa. He'd jumped in to save me, but I had kicked and punched so much he couldn't get a hold on me for the longest time. I broke his nose and gave him a black mask of bruises around his eyes.

Miss Ross wasn't all gloves and cruelty after all. I figured that out the first night I was home from the hospital. I woke up in Mama's bed. I was feverishly hot, so I called out for Papa. The hallway was dark and no one came. I felt the coolness of a breeze drift in from an open window. I got up, then crawled out onto the roof. I was sitting there in my nightgown taking in the cool late-night breeze hoping my eyes would clear up, so I could see the stars. My vision was still blurry from that muddy brown water, but I started to hear voices.

At first, they were all jumbled like my thoughts. I moved closer to the edge of the roof so I was right in the path of the voices as they floated up into the sky from the porch. Papa and Miss Ross were down there chattering away. Papa was pacing back and forth on the porch. I could hear the clomp, clomp of his heavy boots. He was muttering to himself. Miss Ross was saying, "Ivar, it was my fault. I shouldn't have been so hard on her. I scared her off."

"I should have taught her to swim," Papa said. "A girl her age should know how to swim."

"A girl her age who doesn't know how to swim wouldn't jump into a river unless someone drove her there. I drove her into that water."

"No," Papa said, and I had to admit he was right. Miss Ross had been mean. Meaner than any woman I'd met, except for Mama. Mama was meaner. She'd left me. She'd walked away and left me. I ran away from the picnic because my mama didn't want me anymore. I'd almost drowned because of her.

I started to cry. I didn't cry when Mama left because I wanted to believe she was visiting Aunt Sarah. I didn't cry when I realized she'd left with the Sawdust Man. After all, she'd left Papa not me, or so Papa tried to tell me, but I didn't believe that lie anymore. Mama had left us both. She'd walked away from all the people who loved her—me, Papa, Grandma Dee, and Grandpa Jared. She didn't love us. She only loved the Sawdust Man, so I cried.

I heard Papa say, "What's that?"

"Nissa." Miss Ross answered. They both came running. I was clawing at the shingles and crying when they came to the window.

"Nissa." Papa was crying, too. As he clambered onto the roof, I could hear the jagged breaths he was taking beneath his tears. He pulled me into his arms and cradled me.

I clung to him saying, "Mama doesn't love me."

"No, baby." Papa rocked me. "She loves you."

I didn't believe him. No one but Mama herself could make me believe she still loved me. No one could try harder than Papa who just about pulled me inside his heart, just so I might believe him. He tucked me into bed. He set me down in the hollow Mama had made in her mattress after sleeping a thousand nights in the same position. Papa put me on my side, then handed me my doll, Sue Ragston. When he kissed me, he breathed in to smell me. That said he loved me. I know that for truth because it made me feel warm right down to the roots of my heart.

Miss Ross was sitting on the bed right behind Papa. His head was still resting on my forehead and I could see her over his shoulder. Her eyes said she was sad, sad enough to raise a gloveless hand and put it on my papa's shoulder. There was nothing phony about that hand. Her fingers were narrow and furrowed, her nails short and clean, but they looked flaky, like a well-made pie crust. Mama's nails looked like that after she'd worked in the garden all day. The most surprising bit of all was that there wasn't a single wart.

Miss Lara Ross had nice ladylike hands that had done their share of work. She wasn't afraid to let me see them because she wanted Papa to know she cared. My throat was too sore to speak and I couldn't find the words to say what I was feeling, so I hummed a little to let Papa know I was a little happy, a bit glad that Lara Ross could be a real person sometimes.

"You need to rest, Ivar. I'll stay with Nissa." Miss Ross's whisper made me think of nighttime winds that come when everything is calm and quiet just to remind me that nature is still alive and waiting for children like me to come out and play.

Papa looked at her. Even from the side, I could read his thoughts from the tired frown on his face. He was trying to tell her I wouldn't like the idea. He knew I wanted my papa. I did, but he was so tired and it hurt me to see him sitting there with every part of his body drooping.

I patted my mattress to ask him to lie down with me. He

turned then watched me pat my bed again. "Neesay," he said, smiling. He walked around the bed, then crawled in and nestled up to me. He took in another breath of me, and I had to smile.

"I'll tell you a story," Miss Ross said, pulling the cover up over Papa and me.

Papa said, "Go home, Lara. You must be exhausted. I'll take you to the door." He started to rise. I moaned in protest and grabbed his hand.

"No." She held up a hand to stop him. "Let me tell you both a story, then I'll go on my own." Miss Ross didn't seem to need a man to do anything for her. I guess she was a little bit like Mama in that way.

"All right." Papa settled in. "Tell away."

Miss Ross leaned on one arm, then began her story. "I was born in Illinois. My father was working for the railroad. Then he rode the rails all day, checking for problems with the track. If there was any part of the line in need of repair, he called it in from the nearest station, then the company sent out a repair crew. His boss—I can't remember his name, but I know he had a birthmark shaped like a crescent moon under his left eye—he told my daddy he'd done such a good job getting all the rails in Illinois in top shape that he had to send him to Louisiana to find broken rail.

"My mother said Daddy could have sold that line of bull for the price of ice in Siberia. She didn't want to move to Louisiana. She was a midwestern girl born and raised. Daddy was from Mississippi, so he was glad to go down there and be close to home. Not Mother—she hated the heat and the threat of hurricanes. She said Southerners had been mutated by the heat. She used to say that Charles Darwin himself would have declared that Southerners had de-evolved one step closer to sloths to protect themselves from the heat. She swore the heat wouldn't get her. Mother spent every day, dawn to dusk, in her garden, working away to prove that the heat couldn't slow her down."

I started to drift, my body felt dull and heavy. I wanted to hear it all. I wanted to know more about Miss Ross's mama, but Papa was sleeping behind me; I could hear the sawing, in-and-out, sound of his breathing. It would have been so easy to float off to sleep. Miss Ross squeezed my hand. Her fingers were cool and dry like a garden stone left in the shade. I had to look up at her. She was smiling down at me saying, "My mother loved roses too. Hers were all different colors—peach and white, yellow and red, all kinds of pinks." I saw all those beautifully colored buds planted in clouds and had to keep listening. "The only yellow rose in Mother's garden was planted on Mother's Day for her own mother, my Grandma Monica, who died of cancer when I was your age. Grandma Monica loved yellow roses. My mother tended those yellow flowers as if their petals were pure silk. It was her way to keep on loving Grandma Monica, I think.

"When I was sixteen, Bobby Journiette asked for my hand in marriage. I loved him. I wanted to be his wife, but Mother said no. She said I was too young to know what love was. To prove her wrong, I destroyed the thing she loved the most. I used her pruning sheers and clipped that yellow rosebush to pieces. I even dug up the roots and snipped them to bits.

"I left the pieces where they lay and waited for her to find them. I was trying to read on the back porch when she finally found them. I heard her scream. It sounded like someone had tried to pull the life out of her. I knew how wrong I'd been to cut up the rosebush right then. I wanted to run to her. I got as far as the tomato patch where I could see her kneeling in the dirt, clutching the buds to her body, tears streaming down her face, dirt covering her pale blue dress. I ran. I ran in shame for my cruelty. I ran for fear that my mother would never forgive me. I ran in pain because I'd hurt my mother so badly. I was in the grove of oak trees by Sutton's Creek before I could stop running. It had begun to rain, but my whole body felt as if it had broken into hot, jagged pieces that were only held together by my skin. I wanted to throw myself into that swelling creek and let the water wash me away.

"I was thigh deep in the water when I heard my mother yelling. I turned to see my mother running across the field, the car behind her, the door open and steam rising up from the engine.

" 'Jeanie! Jeanie!' she'd yelled.

"I didn't know what to do. Part of me wanted to dive into that cold water and drown before she could touch me. I also wanted her to catch me and beat the guilt out of my heart.

"What she did was rush into the water and hug me. She wrapped her arms around me so tight I thought she was going to break my arms right off. 'I'm sorry, Jeanie. I'm so very sorry.'

" 'What?' I'd gasped.

" 'I didn't know. I had no idea how strongly you felt about Bobby.'

" 'I killed Grandma's roses.'

" 'You sure did.' My mother laughed. She actually laughed." Miss Ross laughed now at the memory.

I cleared my throat to find my voice, then asked, "She didn't love the roses?" The whole story was confusing me so much I had to wake up all the way just to try and figure it out.

"No." Miss Ross shook her head. "My mother loved that rosebush. As she put it, she knew I had to love Bobby an awful lot to ruin something so precious to her."

"But you didn't marry him," I said, unsure of her love for Bobby Journiette who was now, as everyone knew, married to Quincey Belle Forester. They lived out by Sutton's Creek and had eight children. Quincey was wide bellied with their ninth, in fact.

"Well, Bobby didn't love me as much as he said he did. Mother said we could get married on my eighteenth birthday. We were officially engaged and I had his ring on my finger, but he started courting Quincey before I turned seventeen and they were married before I was eighteen."

"Oh," I said, convinced Miss Ross had loved Bobby. I knew then that she probably had stayed unmarried until she got old because she was pining for Bobby Journiette.

"Bobby wasn't the reason I told you this story."

"You had a reason?"

"Yes." She rustled my hair. "I wanted you to see that actions don't change a mother's love."

"What?"

"I ruined my mother's favorite thing and she still loved me."

"I didn't do anything to Mama."

Miss Ross closed her eyes for a second. I think I shocked her. "Well, even though I killed her Grandma rosebush, she still loved me."

"So, you think Mama still loves me?"

"I know she does."

I wanted to believe Miss Ross, but I didn't. She'd told a nice story and meant well, but she wasn't Mama and she didn't even know my mama. She could never tell me what Mama felt or thought.

I was wide awake now and kind of afraid of falling asleep. That nothingness had really rattled me. Papa was there, but he was sleeping, so I wanted Miss Ross to keep talking until I got tired again. "Why'd your mama call you Jeanie?"

"I was named after my father's sister. Mother didn't like her. She hated calling me by her name, so she called me by my middle name, which is Jean."

"That's pretty."

"Thanks," she said, shaking Sue Ragston's fabric hand. "Your mother has a pretty name, too. Where'd it come from?"

"Heirah?" I asked. I was always glad to explain Mama's name. It was real special. "Mama was born January 1, 1900. Grandpa Jared said she was born at the beginning of a great era, so that should be her name. Grandma Dee was sure people would think Mama was a boy with a name spelled E-R-A, so they spelled it different."

"Clever."

I hummed. There was really nothing to say. I thought a moment, then asked, "What was Illinois like?" It was a question to keep her talking. She told me about rolling hills covered with cornfields and treeless miles of land without water. I dreamt of cornfields dotted with yellow rosebushes.

Memories
and Marriages

I WOKE UP TO PAPA'S SINGING. HE WAS SINGING IN Norwegian. I don't understand a word of it, but it sounds like sand when you shake it around in a pail—smooth and rough at the same time. I love to listen to him and imagine what he's saying. When he calls Grandpa Knut from the store, I imagine he's talking about Norway. They remember the mountains of ice and the roads where only sleighs and people on skis could travel. He'd tell Papa how he missed sitting in front of a fire on a cold winter's night—the fierce wind howling at the windows looking for a crack to sneak through, the fire snapping and crackling at the wind to tease it. I hated cold weather, but roasting nuts and fish over a fire sounded grand. Papa said Grandpa Knut and his little brother, Papa's Uncle Erling (who was sixty or so), would tell stories of when they were little boys and they'd cut holes in the ice to go swimming.

The thought of the water made me shiver until my bones felt like they'd gone soft. I tried to listen real hard to Papa's voice so I didn't think about water anymore. It sounded kind of sad, so I followed it. He was out on the little balcony that hangs over the back door. He stopped singing as I walked down the hall and was crying when I came outside.

It looked like the tears hurt as they passed over his bruised and puffy face. I felt so bad about kicking Papa, I wanted to crawl back in bed. He saw me. Turning, he scooped me up and spun around.

"Papa!" I laughed.

Putting me down, he smiled. "I need to hear that laugh." He crouched down to tap my chest. "Know there is happiness in that little heart."

"You don't look happy, Papa." I wiped away a tear, careful not to press a bruise. He took my hand.

"You worry too much, Nissa." He kissed my hand. When he said that, it felt like he closed a door. We weren't together on that balcony anymore. There was him and there was me, but no us. That's what I missed so much about Mama and me. We were a great we.

I wanted that with Papa, so I asked, "What were you singing?"

He stood up and smiled in a way that said he was even farther away and I thought I'd made things worse. Then he said, "It's a fisherman's song. Really, it's a song his family sings to bring him a good catch and wish him a safe journey. My mama used to sing it to me."

As if it was a fact I'd just discovered, it made me tingle inside to realize Papa had lost his mama, too. I felt sad, ashamed, and happy all at one time. Papa knew what it meant to lose a mama. "What was she like?"

"Nissa Ingrid Bergen?" He looked down at me. "She was fire and water fused together."

"Steam."

He laughed. "I guess so. She worked all day fixing nets and keeping house, then she'd sit by the fire at night reading books to us."

"Really? Did she read as well as Mama?"

He bent down and whispered, "Better."

I wasn't sure how that made me feel. It didn't seem right that he should think that anyone was better than Mama, but then I realized it was his mama we were talking about and I smiled. "Do you miss her?"

Papa sat down on the bench by the door, then pulled me into his lap. "When I was little, I missed her so much I'd pretend she was just gone to the marketplace and would be back before dark. As I got older, I thought I'd forget her, then I realized you don't forget people. Sometimes they fade a little—like I can't remember how my mother smelled."

As Papa talked, I prayed to God I'd never forget a thing about Mama, right down to the tiny freckle under her right eye. Papa was saying, "Papa smells of leather, but I don't remember Mama's scent. I do remember the sea blue color of her eyes and the way her fingers felt against my skin— warm, but callused. I remember how much she loved me and Papa and her garden."

"She had a garden?"

"Yes, but Mama favored vegetables over flowers. Her favorite flower was a pumpkin blossom. They're hard to grow in Norway."

"Are our mamas alike?"

Papa sighed. "They're both strong women, but your mama's got a fire all her own."

The way Papa said that with a sense of wonder and pride in his voice told me he still loved Mama. "If Mama came back, would you still be married?"

He didn't answer for the longest time. I held my tongue because I was afraid of what he'd say. When he spoke, it was barely above a whisper, "I'm done with dreams, Nissa. I can't tell you what might be. I can only tell you what is. Your mama isn't here and you and I can't stand still waiting for her to come back. We've got to keep on growing."

"Keep on growing?"

"What? Do you think people get to be adults and they stop growing?"

"I think old people shrink. I've seen a picture of Mrs. Mabel at her front door. She used to be tall enough to block the window, now she's barely tall enough to see into it."

"Nissa." He roughed up my hair. "I didn't mean in the body. I meant up here." He tapped his head, then touched his heart. "And here."

With all the thinking and the wondering about Mama, I felt like I'd plum stretched my heart and mind to their limits. I slouched in his arms. "I was hoping for a rest from all that when I got bigger."

"See what I mean? You worry too much, Nissa." He rubbed my tummy.

He was right. When Mama was around, I worried she'd leave. Now that she was gone, I worried she'd never come back. There was no escaping the worries. What I wanted was a place where I'd know that when I laid my head down to go to sleep, everything would be the same when I got up in the morning. I don't mean that nothing would change.

That'd be awful. The flowers wouldn't bloom. The water-melon wouldn't ripen. Actually, the sun wouldn't even come up. No, I just wanted to know that the people I cared about would be there when I got up—Mama and Papa. And Grandma Dee and Grandpa Jared too—I always knew they were in their beds in Mississippi. I also knew Papa was always there. He'd never leave me. I hugged him tight and wished God would show Mama how to stay in one place—our place.

What I didn't want was to go to sleep knowing somebody else who didn't love me would be in the house when I woke up, but that's just what happened. I slept on and off for two whole days. Drowning takes a lot out of you. On the third morning, I felt good enough to go downstairs for breakfast and who should be there but Miss Ross. I saw her standing in front of the sink with her spiky heels and wrinkle-free dress and I wanted to chop those heels off with a butcher knife so she could have good footing to run right back where she came from, but Papa acted like she belonged there.

He made cornbread pancakes, then served them with brown- sugar syrup and tomato juice because those were my favorite things. He was trying to sweeten me up so I would think Miss Ross belonged there, too, but it didn't work. Miss Ross did her own sort of bribing. She brought sliced peach-es. Papa gave her bowls to put the peaches in.

When the table was ready, I sat down and stared at all the good food. Miss Ross was looking at me as if to ask, "So what'd you bring to the table this morning?"

Since Mama had left, I could switch emotions at the drop of a coin. I'd go from feeling mad to feeling ashamed in a heartbeat. I was getting more and more like Mama every day. Seeing all that food, and their faces, I wasn't mad at Miss Ross for being there anymore. I felt left out. So I jumped up from the table, then ran out yelling, "I'll be right back!"

I heard Papa yell for me, but I was already out the gate. I went down the back alley to Mary Carroll's. Her family had breakfast before dawn because Mrs. Carroll believed families should eat together and Mr. Carroll's shift at the coal mine in Vespers, Mississippi started at 6:00 A.M. Mary usually went back to bed after breakfast, so I went behind the lilac bushes along the side of the house, then skirted my way up to her window.

"Mary!" I tapped on the glass.

"Nissa?" She shouted, pushing the window open. "You aren't dead!"

"Well, you would have known that if you'd come over."

"Ma wouldn't let me. She said it isn't right to visit a sickbed unless the ill person's your relative. You all right?"

I held my arms up and stepped back toward the bushes so she could have a look. "What do you think?"

"You look pale and kind of wrinkled. Were you all pruny when they took you out of the water?"

"How should I know? I was dead to the world when Papa pulled me out."

"Did you really die? Ma said you died. I think that's the real reason she wouldn't let me see you. When somebody comes back from the dead, it's either because God saved them or the devil brought them back to do his dirty work."

I put on my best, "I'm going to get you" face, then charged her with a roar. She squealed, then pulled her head into the house so fast she knocked it against the window. I laughed as she rubbed her head. "I'm no devil child, Mary. It's just me—Nissa."

"Nissa the devil child," Mary said, squinting in pain. "You gave me a goose egg."

"You were being a goosehead with all that devil stuff. I'm not dead. God and Papa made sure of that."

"Good." She leaned out toward me. We hugged as best we could with her hanging out the window and me standing on my tiptoes. "I'm real glad, Nissa."

Before I could ask if she was glad enough to give me some of her mama's yellow roses, she started laughing. "What?" I shouted.

She bit her lip, then said, "Peter Roubidoux's telling folks at school that your skin has turned green and your eyes are all bulged out."

"I should poke him in the eye."

"He's got water on the brain!"

"Yeah." We giggled.

Little Anthony leaned out of the boys' window. "Shush, Ma will hear."

We covered our mouths and laughed some more, then I remembered why I was there. "Can I have a few of your mama's roses?"

"You've got roses at your house."

"Mama cut them down, and I need yellow. Miss Ross brought me peach slices for breakfast, so I want to give her yellow roses."

"What? The water must have sogged up your brain." Mary shook her head. "Meet you in the garden." She was back inside the house before I could yell at her for her soggy-brain crack.

I was the first one out to the garden. Mary came out with a steak knife and started to cut some of the flowers for me, saying, "So, you've decided it isn't bad for your papa to be courting Miss Ross?"

"She's real nice."

"As nice as your ma?"

"My mama wasn't nice." I felt a twinge in my chest when I said it, but it felt good after I let the words go.

"Says who? Your ma never did one cruel thing—to me."

"Well, she left me."

"So, you're mad at her. Ma knew you'd be mad at her one day. You have a right to be mad, she said."

"Your ma never says stuff like that to me. She just asks if I want lemonade or ice water, then smiles."

"You aren't her girl."

"Miss Ross talks to me about all sorts of things."

Mary handed me a bunch of roses. "That's because she wants you to be *her* girl."

I looked down at the roses. I had half a mind to throw them on the ground, but that would've been rude, and Mary had cut them for me and all. "Thanks, Mary," I shouted, running toward the alley.

"Come back later! We'll go grubbing!" I didn't pay much attention to her invitation. I was thinking about Miss Ross. If Mary was right, Miss Ross was trying to become my mama by being nice to me. I almost believed she really liked me, but I wasn't going to let her fool me anymore. No way. No cute little stories about roses and a couple of soggy peaches were going to make her my day-to-day mama. She had something wrong with her brain if she thought she could bribe her way into our family.

I rushed back into the house, threw the roses in her face with a loud, "Here," then stomped off to my room. I heard her and Papa yapping back and forth below as I plopped down on my bed and picked up Sue Ragston. I imagined that the thorns had clawed up Miss Ross's face and that she had become so ugly Papa wanted her to leave at once.

There was a knock at my door a little later. I didn't hear Papa's stair clomping, so I figured it was Miss Ross. I refused to answer it.

"Nissa." It was Papa. He must have been pretty mad to walk up the stairs without making a sound. I was too scared to open the door.

"Nissa, I'm coming in." He opened the door, then walked over to my desk by the window. He turned. "Why did you throw those flowers at Miss Ross?"

Pulling Sue Ragston up under my chin, I said, "I don't want her as my day-to-day mama."

"And that gives you the right to be rude?"

"She's trying to take Mama's place!"

"I'll ask again. That gives you the right to be rude?"

"No."

"Go downstairs and apologize."

"Do I have to?"

Papa pointed at the door. He was so serious he didn't say another word. I did what he told me to. He was right behind me when I came into the kitchen. Miss Ross was sitting at the table with a wet washcloth in her hand. She dabbed her face. It looked so red and sore, her eyes were even watery. For a minute, I thought I'd hurt her bad, then I realized she'd been crying.

Mama says you should never cry over someone you don't like. If Miss Ross thought that way, maybe she really did like me. "I'm sorry, Miss Ross."

She touched one of the roses. She'd put them in a vase and set it on the table. "Yellow roses. That's a real sweet gesture, Nissa." She sniffled. "Why'd you throw them at me?"

"Mary Carroll said you were trying to make me into your little girl." I heard Papa behind me hissing at Mary's name.

Miss Ross laughed. "You don't like the idea of you and me being friends?"

I told her, "A girl and a lady can't be friends. They're niece and aunt or daughter and mother or something like that. Otherwise they're nothing at all."

"Who said that?" Papa asked, sitting down at the kitchen table.

"Nobody. It's just true."

"Are you sure?" Miss Ross asked.

"Well, did you have any lady friends when you were a girl?" I slid onto my chair.

"Hmmm." Miss Ross looked at Papa. He was eating his pancakes cold. She said to me, "There was Mrs. Baker, my piano teacher. I'd say we were friends."

"She was your teacher and you were her student. You weren't friends."

"Right." Miss Ross shook her head. I had her there. It was true. The only reason she wanted to be my friend was so she could marry my papa and be my new day-to-day mama. "So, we have to be enemies?" she asked.

"No." I thought about it for a second. "I didn't say that, but you really don't want to be my friend. You want to be nice to me only so you can marry my papa."

Miss Ross's face grew darker than the tomato juice. "Heavens."

Papa laughed. "Spoken like Heirah's one-and-only daughter."

"Heavens!" Miss Ross covered her eyes with her glove-less hands. "Is she always like this?"

"All year round," Papa said, laughing.

Miss Ross asked him, "Her embarrassing honesty doesn't bother you?"

"Neesay and her mother are usually right on the mark. You can't be ashamed of honesty like that. If you are, you're hiding from something you shouldn't be."

Miss Ross blushed. "Are you hinting that I want to marry you?" It was as if I'd vanished. They were talking like I wasn't even there. I didn't matter, it was a great way to eavesdrop without leaving the room. I wanted to know how the conversation turned out.

"Well, do you?" Papa asked her.

Miss Ross bowed her head. "Mr. Bergen, you should be ashamed of yourself!"

"Lara, if you're not interested in being my wife, then what are you doing here at seven in the morning with a jar of sliced peaches?"

"Nissa's been ill. You've been overworked and worried. I thought it would be a nice gesture to help you out."

"I see." Papa nodded, trying to hide his smile by biting his lips.

Miss Ross took a deep breath. "Well, by having me here, aren't you expressing some interest in me." She didn't look Papa in the eye.

"Well, wouldn't it be rude to put you out on the street when you're being so nice to Nissa and all?"

They were playing games with each other and I didn't like it. Papa couldn't marry anybody. He was married to Mama. And her being away for six months didn't change that one bit. Even if she was gone a zillion years, he'd still be married to her.

"You're teasing me now, Ivar," Miss Ross said, looking Papa in the eye. She was a husband stealer and stupid. Mama would have been all over Papa by this time, making him laugh until he staggered.

"Indeed I am. Let's eat." Papa sat down and Miss Ross joined us for breakfast.

My heart was pounding out the tune to "Anything Goes." I couldn't believe my papa was talking about marriage in our kitchen over cornbread pancakes and tomato juice. He had no right to do that. He couldn't just trade wives! I didn't want some strange woman coming into our house, cooking our meals, cleaning the rooms, and planting flowers in our garden. I watched with my fists clenched hoping Miss Ross would slap him in the face for even suggesting she marry him, then walk out and never come back. But Papa and Miss Ross seemed happy over the whole thing, smiling at each other and all. I wished they'd choke on those darn peaches.

Grandma Dee

A<small>LL THE TALK OF MARRIAGE MADE ME THINK</small> P<small>APA WAS DOING</small> it to keep Mama away. After all, if she came back and saw Papa with another woman, she'd be so mad, she'd never speak to us. Then again, maybe he was just getting even. Mama ran off with the Sawdust Man, so Papa found himself Miss Ross. It all seemed so mean. I felt like my family was at war. In the end, the losing side would be mine. Mama had her Sawdust Man. Papa had Miss Ross. Who was left for me? No one. It was unfair and downright lonely.

Papa must have known I was lonely because he sent for Grandma Dee so she could spend Christmas with us. I suppose that was a good sign. If he talked to Mama's mama that must mean he still wanted Mama to be a part of our family. He telephoned Grandma Dee from Minkie's Mercantile and told her I drowned and needed my grandma. She was on the next train to Harper. Papa thought it was best if we all went to meet her at the station so she knew right off that I was okay. Standing on the platform staring at the empty tracks and listening to Papa and Miss Ross whisper to each other, I couldn't help thinking about the word *we*.

If I'm waiting in line to use the bathroom at school and there's another girl behind me when a teacher comes up to ask what's going on, I don't say, "We're waiting for the bathroom." It's true, but I'm not about to join up with some girl wiggling in her stockings if I don't even know her.

Papa didn't smile when he said "we" should all go to the train station to meet Grandma Dee, but that's because he was worried about talking to Mama's mama. He ought to have been ashamed of himself for letting things get to the point where Mama wasn't included in his "we" anymore. It used to be that when Papa got up in the morning and decided it was a good day for a picnic, he'd stand on the back steps and stretch, then turn toward the house and shout "*We* should go on a picnic!" By "we," he meant Papa, Mama, and Nissa. But when he said "we" should all go to the train station to meet Grandma Dee, his "we" meant Papa, Nissa, and Miss Ross. I didn't like the idea that Mama had slipped right out of the Bergen family we.

Mama was gone for scarcely seven months and Papa was planning to replace her. It all left me in a five-hundred-pound funk. I'm sure sadness has weight because when I'm in a funk, it feels like my soul gets heavier. The sadder I am, the harder it is to move because the sadness gets so heavy.

The morning Grandma Dee arrived, I felt like my sorrow weighed more than all the slouching bags of grain at the end of the platform. My mama was gone because she didn't love me anymore and my papa was in love with somebody else. It was as if all the love had seeped right out of our family. The Bergen family had fallen apart and I was the only one left standing there staring at the tracks waiting for Grandma Dee.

The train was in a furious hurry when it finally showed up. It was howling in a mad rush as it chugged around the bend. I could swear the grill was trying to chew up the track as it approached the station. The engine pulled the train in so fast the first two passenger cars slid right on by the platform, the wheels below them screeching and spitting sparks.

When I saw Grandma Dee step off the train only a couple of feet from Papa, I imagined she'd been sitting in her seat with her fists clenched in concentration to will that train to stop smack-dab in front of us. Grandma Dee was a powerful woman who could do whatever she wanted. She carried her strength in broad shoulders that required hand-tailored shirts. Her jaws were so tight they could have been used for a builder's square. She was as tall as Papa. She could look him straight in the eye when they stood facing each other. Mama used to say Grandma Dee could have been a man if she didn't have a place to carry babies and such gentle blue eyes and long lashes, things no man would have.

"Baby Nee!" Grandma Dee bent at the knees to open her arms to me. I was too heavy to run, so I walked to her. "Are you still sick, Nissa?"

I hugged her, hoping she'd know from the way I held her that I wanted everything to go back to the way it used to be when Mama was home and Grandma Dee came to help her turn our cucumbers into pickles and our tomatoes into juice. Grandma Dee pulled back and touched my forehead with her palm. She asked Papa, "Is she ill, Ivar?"

Papa scooped me up. "Neesay's suffering from sadness." He kissed me on the cheek.

"It's all too much for a young girl." Grandma Dee patted my back. "Too much. Let's get her home."

We started to walk back to the house. With my head on Papa's shoulder, I could see Miss Ross. She didn't look too much like she felt as if she was part of the family. She was staring straight ahead. Her skin was pale and moist. She looked like she'd been carved out of a sad, peach wax. Grandma Dee hadn't even said hello and Papa hadn't introduced her. I lifted my head and looked at Grandma Dee. "Grandma."

"What, Sweetie?"

"This is Miss Lara Ross." I leaned back and pointed at Miss Ross.

Grandma nodded in her direction. "How do."

"I'm sorry," Papa blushed. "Lara Ross, this is Heirah's mother, Delia Russell."

Miss Ross squeezed his arm, then smiled at Grandma Dee. "Nice to meet you, Mrs. Russell," she whispered. Grandma just nodded.

Papa put me in Mama's bed when we got home. He knew how much I loved her smell in the pillows. If I had to lose Mama, I never wanted to lose the soury-sweet smell of hard water and vinegar Mama left behind on her pillow.

Grandma Dee sat sewing in the window seat. The sunlight coming in from behind her cast shadows over the front of her like a dark gray shawl. I could see her raise her hand over her shoulder as she pulled a thread taut. Grandma Dee had sewn everything—from the red-and-white checkered curtains in her outhouse to the velvety covers on our living room chairs.

With her face hidden in a shadow, I felt safe enough to say, "You told me Mama still loves me."

"And she does."

"That's a lie."

Grandma Dee didn't respond. Her hand didn't rise above her shoulder to make another stitch. She was silent, but I could hear the quiet wheezing in her breath, then she said, "If you think your mama doesn't love you anymore, then you're a fool, Nissa. Your mistake is that you confuse love and devotion."

I rose up on my elbow to listen carefully. "What do you mean?"

"Love is a feeling and it drives you to do many crazy and wonderful things, but it doesn't make you loyal. Devotion's what makes you stay."

"Mama isn't loyal?"

"She never has been, Nissa. I knew it for a fact the first time she called another woman 'Mama.'"

"What?"

"Heirah's always fallen in love at the first kind gesture. When one of our neighbors invited her over for a little bread pudding and cinnamon tea, Heirah was ready to trade me in for a new mama. By the time she was twelve, Heirah was calling twenty different women in the neighborhood 'Mama.' Having one mother just wasn't enough for her."

"So, she needs a new daughter because I'm not enough?"

"Good Lord." Grandma Dee's laugh was a nervous flutter. "Did I say that? I should cut my tongue right out. Nissa, you have to believe that your mother still loves you. You haven't done anything wrong. It's your mama. Heirah Rae's got a hole in her that nobody can fill."

"How'd it get there?" I asked, imagining a dark hole in my mother's heart, like the mouth of a cave—empty, scary, and unfillable. Mama had her hands over it and tears running down her face. She looked so sad, it made my chest hurt.

Grandma Dee said, "I don't know. Your grandfather and I gave Heirah everything we had and so did your papa."

"Maybe Papa should have given her another baby."

Grandma Dee moved over to the bed. I lay back as she raised the covers to tuck me in. "Your parents tried to have a new baby since the moment you were born. Your mama was pregnant, too, a few times, but the babies died."

"Like Benjamin?"

"Yes, honey. Like Benjamin."

"Why did the babies die?"

"I don't think I should be talking to you about these things. Children shouldn't be thinking about death." Grandma Dee patted my chest. "You put all those thoughts out of your head. You remember your mama loves you. That's the only thing you need to know. I think you should get some rest now. Dream of your mama loving you."

Grandma Dee left the room. I tried to remember Mama loving me, but I could only see her crying over the hole in her heart. She was sitting on a bench below the Catalina cherry tree in the garden with her knees curled up to her chest and her housecoat hanging down to the ground. I'd seen Mama there, sitting like that, a few months ago. I was going to go out to her and whisper soft words in her ear as she always did for me when I was sad, but I got scared. I was frightened by the spot on her housecoat. As the fabric shifted in the wind, I saw a red stain on it. Blood. I knew it was blood and it scared me. When Mama bled she was mean. Awful mean.

When I was five, she started to bleed while we were picking cherries in the garden and I thought she'd kill me. We were running around the tree, stepping up onto the benches to jump for a cherry, then hopping down to run to the bench on the other side of the tree. I really wasn't tall enough to reach the cherries, but it was great fun to chase Mama up and down those benches. Sometimes when she stopped to jump for cherries, I'd run right into her and knock her down. It was fun to see her scramble to land on her feet without spilling the cherries. She laughed when she fell, too, even if she fell to her knees and we had to pick the cherries up off the ground.

One time, I was running to catch up to her when I saw blood spotting the back of her dress. I stopped short, but I still bumped into her. She laughed, then jumped to the ground with a handful of cherries, saying, "Better try harder if you want to knock me off, Nissa."

She looked back at me as I yelled, "You're bleeding, Mama!" I pointed to her dress.

"What?" She twisted around to look. Seeing the blood, she screamed so shrilly I thought she'd break something in her throat.

"What's wrong?" I asked.

"You did this!" she shouted. I believed her. With all the jumping and the jostling we'd done, I'd probably cut her with the metal basket I was holding.

"You did this." Mama was squeezing the cherries in her hand, the red juice oozing out between her fingers.

"I'm sorry, Mama."

"Sorry?" She took a step toward me, her bare feet slapping against the flagstones as she raised her arm, then hurled the crushed cherries at me. Screaming, she charged forward, flinging cherries. I ran. I didn't know what else to do. If Mama didn't have to get over the bench, she would have caught me for sure. And with the way she was yelling and throwing, I thought she was going to hurt me and hurt me bad.

Papa came running into the garden as I reached the house. He went straight for Mama who wailed and clawed as he hugged her with his arms held tightly over hers. "Heirah Rae, Heirah Rae," Papa gasped, trying to quiet her down.

Ashamed of what I'd done, I hid under the hall table. From there, I watched Papa lift Mama, then carry her through the back gate. Blood had covered the back of her dress. I was sure Mama was dying and I'd killed her. I couldn't move from that spot. I sat there shaking until my muscles ached, thinking I'd murdered my mama.

Mrs. Carroll came over to watch me. She told me Mama would be fine. Crouching down in front of the table, she tried to tell me I had not hurt her. "Something inside her broke, Nissa. The doctors will fix it and she'll be fine."

The skirt of her pink dress lying on the floor in odd little ripples, reminding me of the cherry frosting on her cakes, I wanted to believe Mrs. Carroll. I wanted to believe that Mama was okay, but I'd seen the blood, I'd done the pushing and the shoving. "I cut her. I hurt Mama."

"No, you didn't, Nissa." Mrs. Carroll reached out her hand. She was crying. The handkerchief she held was all crinkled up and wet. It was only a cloth, but it looked as if it was in pain and it scared me.

"Go away!" I screamed.

She didn't move, so I screamed again. I screamed until Mrs. Carroll stood up and walked away, then I yelled again to keep her from coming back and everything else disappeared. I don't know if I'd fainted or if my memory has a blank spot, but the next thing I remember was Mama cradling me. We were on the floor of the hall. Mama was rocking me back and forth and whispering in a lullaby tune, "My baby, Nissa. My baby, Nissa. My perfect little girl."

Papa was kneeling behind her, rubbing her shoulders, touching her wilted hair. "Heirah, let's put her to bed."

I should have been happy. I should have felt safe, but I felt heavy and large in Mama's arms. It was almost as if I were the wrong person to be there.

Drowning for Real

DREAM-REMEMBERING THE MOMENT WHEN I DIDN'T FIT IN my mother's arms, I knew what Grandma Dee had meant. I wasn't enough for Mama. She needed a baby to hold in her arms, a warm, powder-smelling baby who was tiny, who needed her and could never hurt her. I was too big, too old, too dangerous to be her baby anymore.

I curled into a ball and prayed to God to make me into a baby again. It didn't work. I fell asleep and when I woke up, I was still a tall, dangerous eleven-year-old. I also felt stiff, too stiff to move. I lay there wishing I could turn into dandelion tufts and blow away in the wind.

Papa leaned in the door. "Are you up for some supper? Grandma Dee made catfish and hush puppies."

"What was I like when I was a baby, Papa?"

Papa laughed as he came into the room. He sat down on the edge of the bed and said, "Fat. You were a pudgy baby." He tickled me. "Your grandfather was so proud."

"Grandpa Jared?"

"No, Knut. My papa." He leaned back and stretched out his arms to make himself big like he always said

Grandpa Knut was. "She's a fine girl. Fine. Fat as a *bjornunge*."

"A *bjornunge*?" I laughed. I had no idea what it meant, but it sounded funny.

"That's a bear cub. A roly-poly, fuzzy baby bear!" He growled as he tickled me. I was screaming with laughter by the time he finally stopped.

"Did Mama like me fat?"

"She loved it. Every fat little roll. She said it gave her more skin to bathe, pinch, and tickle."

"She wanted more babies like me?"

"Yes." He tapped my nose.

"Why didn't she have them?" I started to think that Mama would have stayed if there had been more babies in the house.

Papa took a deep breath. "Your grandmother said you'd asked her that question this morning."

"I want to know."

"You always do. One of these days, your head's going to get too full with all the things you have to know." He tapped my forehead.

"Please."

Papa sighed. "Do you remember Benjamin?"

"He was so small Mama had to borrow my doll clothes to dress him." I thought of a tiny, wiggly baby in Sue Ragston's brown dress with the orange and yellow daisies, his feet kicking the skirts around, his tiny fists hiding in the cuff ruffles; he would have been the prettiest little boy around.

"Yes." Papa nodded, but he didn't smile like Mama

had when she'd told me that story. "Do you know what happened to him?"

"He got a sickness in his lungs and he was too small to fight it off."

"That's right. What did you do when he died?"

"I cried?" I asked, because I couldn't remember. I was only three.

"You cut off all of your hair, then tried to bury yourself because you knew we'd put Benjamin in the ground to rest forever."

"I did?"

"You did."

"I don't remember it." I thought of myself running into the woods across the railroad tracks and finding a mound of moist, red dirt where I could dig until it coated my hands, then lying down in the hole I'd dug and burying myself. That dirt would feel so cool, but it would scare me. I wouldn't want all that dark weight on top of me. I prayed Benjamin didn't know he was dead and buried. I hoped he was a bare-butt little angel floating around the clouds with a little harp. Sounds silly I suppose, but babies would love to fly. They get so happy when you throw them up in the air. Mary's brother, Jessup, could be mad enough to bite and you toss him up in the air and he's giggly by the time you catch him. I see Benjamin as a giggling angel playing music for God.

"Well, your mama and I remembered it and we were afraid you'd be just as sad if you knew Mama's other babies died. So, we decided not to talk about any of the other babies until after you'd grown up some—"

"What other babies?"

Papa didn't answer for a moment. He looked scared. Finally, he closed his eyes and said, "Your mama lost two babies before they were born—one when you were five and the other just this past winter."

"That's why Mama went to Aunt Sarah's? She lost a baby?"

"Yes."

"Her baby died?"

"Yes."

"Why?"

"No one knows." He squeezed my hand. "Sometimes babies die."

It wasn't just sometimes. It was because I hit Mama that time we were picking cherries. I'd killed Mama's baby. I killed the baby. I started to cry and I wished Papa had never found me in that muddy old river.

"Don't cry, honey." Papa lifted me up, but I fought him. No murderer deserves a hug. He shifted his arms to keep his grip and I threw myself to the side. I fell right to the floor. I was up and running before Papa could turn around. I heard him running after me as I pushed past Miss Ross to get out the front door. I could hear the gravel crackling under my feet as I ran down Main Street, heading for the woods. I wanted to find the river and drown myself—this time for real.

It was getting dark. Everything looked gray. It was hard to stay up as I jumped and tripped through the underbrush. I could hear branches snapping behind me as Papa entered the woods calling my name. I heard rushing water, so I turned to find it. I started down a hill, then lost my footing on the moss-covered ground. I screamed as I twisted and tumbled my way toward the water. The bushes clawed at me as I rolled, slowing me down for an instant until I broke through them. The rush and crunch of leaves filled my ears. On pure instinct, I screamed as loud as a rusted windmill, then I realized I had nothing to fear. I was doing just the right thing if I wanted to drown in the river and sink into the cool mud at the bottom until I was dead and buried.

I fell silent, then splashed down into the water. I lay there on my back with the water lapping at my ears, feeling the pain of bruises stinging my flesh. I was in the shallow rapids of Sutton's Creek perched on a bed of slimy rocks. And suddenly, I felt stupid.

Papa was tearing through the brush above me, screaming. I couldn't do anything right. I'd run off to drown myself for the sin of killing a baby, but I was wallowing in the shallows of Sutton's Creek instead and I'd hurt Papa at the same time. I never meant to hurt him.

The best thing I could do was disappear, run away and never be seen again. Mama could go off and have her babies. Papa and Miss Ross could be newlyweds like April had always wanted to be. I got up from the rocks and ran, remembering how April said that newlyweds go off all by themselves to pretty places like Niagara Falls or Wisconsin Dells. They spend their time in the fragrant mists of falling water and do baby making until they fall into a dreaming sleep. Papa needed the time to sleep. He worried too much about me. Lately, I'd noticed that his eyes seemed to be wandering into the back of his head while he was reading the *Tucumsett Gazette*.

If I was gone, Papa wouldn't worry anymore. Then again, Mama was gone and I worried about her all the time. I didn't take a breath without thinking about Mama. Ready to run all the way to Chicago if I had to, I kept running away from the creek until I ran out of air.

I stopped. All my crazy thinking had me twisted up tighter than a lynching knot. Grandpa Jared once said your thoughts are only worth where they take you. The things I'd been thinking had me standing in the middle of a clearing among bent, drooping trees draped in Spanish moss. I tried to find stars I knew that would tell me which direction I was facing, but the dense branches reached across the clearing, so I could barely see the night sky. I stared into the forest, hoping I could see a path, but I only saw the dark forms of bushes along the ground. I couldn't help but think that only God knows how many dirty, hungry, hairy beasts were hiding in the dark woods around me.

Listening, I couldn't hear Papa, only the shrill chants of the cicada who seemed to be cheering on the animals I couldn't see. I was afraid to stand out in the open for fear I'd be charged by one of the wild boars that had gored Mr. Cassell's son, Matthew, then left him bloody and broken with only half a stomach to eat with. The trees seemed so drippy and dark they could be hiding snakes or possum. There was no safe place in the entire woods.

I ran in one direction, thinking I was headed for the creek. The hoot of an owl stopped me with the hollow, haunting question, "Whooo, whooo, whooo's behind you?"

Knowing owls don't hunt near the water, I turned around and ran the other way. I could have been going north, south, east, or west for all I knew. I could have been going straight up and I wouldn't have known the difference. The trees were crowding out the sky. I couldn't have found the North Star with a telescope. Not that it would have done me any good. I never did figure out if our house was north or south of the woods at the end of Main Street. All I knew was that we were three doors down from the livery for Mr. Cassell's hotel and catty-corner from Mr. Minkie's Mercantile which was sandwiched between the post office and the feed store. I would've given a pint of blood to be sitting in front of Mr. Minkie's old Franklin stove with an itchy wool blanket over my shoulders and a hand-warming cup of coffee sweet with heavy cream and honey, Papa telling stories about winter in Norway. Papa. He would get me out of the woods. He had followed the loggers into the giant forests of Skein. He could find me and take me home. I screamed for him.

It's strange how the sound of an insect echoes in the night like the trembling in an owl's hoot. I could hear a twig snap and the sound seemed to bounce off the forest floor, but my shout was swallowed before it had the time to travel past the nearest tree. I yelled again, then listened, but I couldn't hear Papa.

I wanted to cry. I longed to throw myself down on the forest floor and bawl. I was fixing to drop down when I heard the crunch-crumbling of something moving through the brush. I crouched down and listened. If it was Papa, he would've been calling my name. Praying I wasn't about to be torn flesh from bone by a panther, I listened extra hard. The crunching was regular: *crunch-crunch-crunch-crunch*. It was like something was walking in Morse Code and saying, "I'm looking. I'm looking." I heard four distinct footsteps like those of a spirited pony. I looked up half-expecting to see the bouncing mane of a white horse, but instead I saw the flashing lights of lanterns. Afraid I was about to be overcome by moonshiners, I ducked down again.

A moment later, I heard a voice. "I'm telling you, Merle, the girl's as nuts as her mama." It was Clem Thibodeaux and his brother, Merle. Seeing them, I realized Grandma Dee had probably sent half the town out looking for me.

Clem kept talking, "I don't know how Bergen puts up with them. If they were my kin, I'd have them committed. Locked up."

Merle didn't answer. He never did. He'd lost his voice when a baseball had hit him square in the Adam's apple when he was still a boy. Ever since then, his brother Clem did enough talking for the both of them.

As far as I was concerned, they could both keep their yaps shut instead of talking about my family that way. Crazy! What's crazy is two grown men living in the same rooms they grew up in doing all the cooking and the cleaning. They were both too particular to find women brave enough to be their wives. Clem was jealous—that's all. Papa had a wife—practically two—and old Clem didn't. I wasn't about to let those oddballs bring me home saying how brave they were to find me.

I went back the way they'd come, knowing it was the route home. If I kept walking in that direction, I was sure to reach the town edge of the woods, but I hadn't traveled far before I saw two more lanterns winding their way between the trees. More searchers, more nosy townspeople talking about my family as if they knew us, as if they'd actually been to our house, seen our lives up close where things are real— Mama helping me read *The Five Little Peppers* as we sit in her window seat, Papa fixing the squeaky hinges on our doors with a tiny tin oil can, and the three of us sitting down to a meal, our hands joined in prayer, heads bowed, and steam rising off the green beans and pot roast to warm our faces.

I ducked behind a tree. The feet heading toward me were walking in rubber. I could hear the warbly jiggle of rubber boots; then came the voices, chattering voices like mockingbirds fighting.

"A fright. A pure fright," one voice said. It was a woman, I could be sure, but I didn't know who. "To almost lose your child. I can't imagine it. Then to have her run off like this." The shrill end of her sentence told me it was our neighbor, Mrs. Dayton. She had the real weight of worry in her voice. She always gave the end of her sentences a shrill note like a whistle when she was worried.

"I think the drowning broke her. With her mama running off and her papa cozying up to Lara Ross, she was bound to lose her mind." Chessie Roubidoux—I'd recognize that pretend-to-be-a-preacher voice anywhere. I was hoping she'd step right into a panther's den and slip right into hell scratching and clawing the dirt all the way down.

I pressed against a tree, feeling the moist bark on my cheek. The ladies passed and I felt safe. I had to find Papa, save him from all these crazy people. They only wanted to find me so they could prove we weren't a good family, show the whole town that Papa had his hands more than full with crazy Heirah's crazy daughter.

I wasn't crazy and Papa was the best father around, even if he thought he could replace Mama with the likes of Miss Ross. I started to move, but I saw more lanterns, so I ducked back behind the tree. I was so concerned about the people coming head on, I didn't hear the footsteps behind me until they were inches away. I spun around and was face to face with the lantern Miss Ross carried. She gasped. "Shh! They're coming," I said.

"Who? Who are you hiding from?" she whispered, turning down the wick on her lantern.

"I don't know. There are people everywhere. Who are they?"

"Your grandmother went straight to the veterans' club and now the whole town is out here blabbering away like it's an Easter egg hunt."

I giggled. Miss Ross could actually be funny sometimes.

"You all right?" she asked, rubbing my back.

I bowed my head. I'd been such a fool. I was just foolish, not crazy.

"What spooked you so?" Miss Ross whispered, as a part of the search party turned toward us.

I thought about it for a minute, but there was no way I could tell her what I'd done. "Papa. Where's Papa?"

"In these woods hunting for you without so much as a match." Miss Ross shook her head.

"I have to find him." I ran off.

Miss Ross followed. The light from her lantern allowed her to keep up. I ran, hoping I'd find him somehow. I don't know why I believed our connection as father and daughter was strong enough to lead me to him, but I did. I just kept going, thinking I'd walk right into him.

Trudging through the brush in high heels, Miss Ross caught up with me and grabbed my arm. "We can't find him in here. The best we can do is go home and let the others know you're all right. They'll find him."

"No." I pulled away.

"It's dark. It's damp. You can't stay out here. You'll get sick."

"I hope I get sick," I shouted, pulling away from her. I started to walk away, mumbling to myself, "I made Papa go out into the woods in the dark. I made Mama go. I made her baby die." Miss Ross stumbled as she tried to pull me back to the house. She fell and I ran off.

She came after me, shouting, "Wait!" She cut in front of me. Holding me by the shoulders, she asked, "What did you say?"

"I killed the baby. I killed the baby."

"What baby?"

"Mama had a baby inside her and I killed it when we were picking cherries. I banged into her with my pail and the baby died."

"That's not true," Miss Ross whispered in my ear. I heard a quiet night wind blowing through my body saying, "Sweetheart, the baby didn't die because of you."

"Then why?" I screamed, stepping back.

There was a faint sizzling sound behind us. I paid no attention, but Miss Ross looked back. Her lantern had fallen over. She righted it in a flourish of panic.

"Why?" I shouted, angry that she'd worry about her stupid lantern when I needed to know, *had* to know why those poor babies had to die.

"Sometimes . . ." She rubbed her hands together. They looked blue gray in the darkness. They must have been so cold. "Sometimes a baby gets sick even before it's born, so sick they can't grow anymore and they die."

"Mama's baby was sick? Sick like Benjamin?"

"Benjamin?"

"My baby brother. He got sick and died."

Miss Ross turned her head, but kept her eyes on me. It made them look small, almost cruel. "Your mother lost two babies?"

"Three counting the one this winter." I told Miss Ross because I wanted someone to mourn those babies, someone to know why my mama was so sad.

"That would drive any woman mad."

"My mama isn't mad!" I pushed Miss Ross to the ground. She got right back up. I heard footsteps. Looking around, I saw the flash of lanterns charging in on us from all directions. I wanted to scream, but they were screaming for me, each one of the townspeople yelling out my name until I couldn't hear a single sound. Then I saw Papa. He pushed past Jonah Hess and came tearing toward me.

"Neesay." He slid toward me, muttering in Norwegian. I'd never learned my father's tongue, but I knew he was grateful. I knew he was glad to have me in his arms, so glad he kissed me until my skin felt raw.

Watermelon

THE NEXT MORNING, I WOKE UP IN A STRANGE PLACE THAT smelled. I opened my eyes to see lace curtains turned into hanging rosettes in the sunlight—loopy yellow cookies turned white with sugar. The smell wasn't anything so sweet as a rosette. It was the smell of sweat mixed with the scent of green-apple suckers.

I lifted my head hoping to find suckers, but I found Miss Ross instead. She was sleeping on the arm of the couch and I was lying in her lap. I rolled off the couch, then stumbled to my feet. It was such an ugly shock to wake up in her lap in what had to be her ugly, lacy living room. She even had little frilly yarn things on the arms of her couch which, at the moment, she was drooling on. Miss frilly, glove-wearing, careful-eater, lacy-curtain Ross was drooling like a dog.

I had to laugh. I laughed so loud she woke up with a fluttering-eye where-am-I? look. "What? Nissa? Nissa, are you all right?" She wiped her face without blushing. "You okay?"

I stopped laughing to think about it. I had nothing to laugh about. "Where are Papa and Grandma Dee?"

"Your father's upstairs and your grandmother is at your house."

I looked around at all the polished furniture and sparkly glass trinkets. "Why are we here?"

"We came out here so everyone would just leave us alone. Your grandmother stayed behind to guard the fort."

"What do people want?" I asked, approaching a table cluttered with crystal animals. I knew the townspeople couldn't keep their noses out of our business, but I couldn't understand why.

"To give your father a piece of their old-fashioned minds." Miss Ross stood up, then tried to pull the wrinkles out of her dress. "Everyone in town has their own ideas about how your father should live his life." She turned her attention to the couch, trying to smooth out the pale green cushions.

"What do they think he should do?"

"Nissa, I really don't think we should discuss this."

"Because you're a stranger?" I asked, turning the glass elephant to chase the lion.

"No, because these are adult issues. I think that's part of the problem here. Too many people giving you adult problems to worry about. You should be enjoying your childhood." Miss Ross obviously thought it was just fine for *her* to offer me old-fashioned advice.

"It's hard to be a child when your mama leaves you."

"Especially if your mother always treated you like an adult."

I wasn't sure just what she meant, but I didn't like the "I'm better" tone in her voice. "Don't say bad things about my mother." I clenched the elephant in my fist, then took a step forward.

"Nissa." Miss Ross's knees buckled a little as she held her hands out to me. "Let me have that."

Having her ask for the elephant made me realize it was raised in the air and I had to ask myself how it got there.

"This is what I'm talking about, Nissa." She took the elephant. "You've got too many worries for a young girl. Worries that make you angry and scared. Think of all the things that have happened to you since your mother's been gone."

Miss Ross moved toward me. It's strange how someone can seem so different in just the time it takes for a cloud to shade the sun. A lady's bones can seem larger than the skin that covers them. Her eyes can suddenly look more black than gray and her voice can carry the weight of gravel when it used to travel like wind.

"You screamed and nearly caused your father to wreck the car. You nearly drowned yourself. You gathered roses, then threw them in my face. Your grandmother came to see you and you ran away in the middle of the night." I backed toward the window as she came forward, listing all the things I'd done. I felt as though I were shrinking. I was already smaller than the chair I hid next to and she only knew half the things I'd done. Had she known that I wanted to poison her with salty lemonade for loving my father, or that my mother didn't love me, or that I thought about baby making, adultery, and murder, she would have squashed me until I was as tiny as those glass animals, and then the lion would eat me up whole.

Maybe I *was* crazy. I tried to hide behind the chair, but

Miss Ross bent down and took my hand before I could move. Her touch was warm and sweaty. Real in a way only a sweaty hand can be when it's squeezing yours and you're thinking you're nuts.

"Everything you've done is understandable. All of it." She smiled, and in a flash, I was looking into gray eyes with little flecks of green, and pupils that looked as if they knew everything that had ever passed through my mind. Seeing the tight lines under her eyes told me she was worried, but the smile said everything would be all right. "I'd be half crazy myself if I was in your place. What you need is a different way to get your feelings out."

I didn't know what to say, so I just listened. "Come with me." Miss Ross led me through her house. She had hardwood floors that were so shiny they reflected the sunlight onto the walls and made the entire place look white. It was like walking through clouds of light. I was off in a dream cloud as she was talking. "When my father got so mad the veins in his face bulged like snakes, he'd go out back and make wood chips. Some men chopped wood, he splintered a single log into tiny chips. He said it made him feel better."

She led the way into the kitchen, then pointed to a chair by the table. "Sit here."

I sat down as she went to her icebox. "I tried it once. When I was sixteen, my father told me I couldn't attend meetings with the agricultural club anymore because I was only going to flirt with the boys." She rubbed her arms. "I had to stop because I nearly cut my toe off with the axe." She wiggled her foot in the air and I had to smile. "When I put the axe down, my arms felt like they were on fire."

She opened the icebox, then took out a watermelon. Carrying it on her arms like a sick feeder pig, she went out the back door. "Come on."

I followed her. The sun wasn't as powerful outside as it had been in her house. It felt natural and warm, but not as magical as it had been inside. Miss Ross set the melon down on the ground, then said, "Have at it."

"What?"

She jumped up, then came down with her feet flat and her hands in fists. "Stomp on it!" Pumping her arms she added, "Tear it up! Let it have the works!"

I was ready to just watch her wiggle and squirm like a mad dog. "You want me to jump up and down on your watermelon?"

"That's right."

"I'd rather eat it."

"Then I'll go to Minkie's and buy us another one for later. This one's going to meet its end right here under the hands of Nissa, Queen of the Vikings—the giants of Norway."

I knew about the Vikings. They were the Norwegian men who were so big and strong the rest of Europe thought they were giants. Papa told me Leif Ericksson had beaten Columbus to the Americas by a couple hundred years because he was so big and fearless. Being a Viking queen would be good. Even better than being the Duchess of Skein. I wanted to be so large and muscular that I feared nothing. I wanted the strength to hold a sword that weighed fifty pounds and row a boat across an ocean. No one could hurt me, no one could run away. I felt invincible and ready to pound that watermelon into slushy little pieces.

I jumped on the melon with both feet. For a fraction of a second, I saw myself slipping on it as if it were a wet barrel and I was the fool trying to stay on it. Just like the men at the St. Patty's Day Festival on the creek. But then I sunk ankle deep into the soft, sweet fruit. Yanking my feet out, I started to stomp on it.

Miss Ross was cheering me on, "Get it, Nissa!"

I dropped to my knees and cracked into the rind. It snapped and I imagined myself breaking up Mama's precious jewelry box; the juice streaming off my hands was her fancy, stupid pearls. I saw Miss Ross's feet and knew Mama wasn't the only one who deserved a little watermelon in the eye. Spinning on one knee, I let Miss Ross have it with the biggest, wettest glob of watermelon I could throw at her.

"Nissa!" she squealed, then bent down to grab her own ammunition.

She picked up a big piece of melon and was about to throw it at me when Papa popped his head out of the upstairs window. His hair was bristly from sleeping and his shirt collar was still unbuttoned as he called down, "What's going on down there?"

I tossed the clump in my other hand at him, but it only made it to the light above the screen door. Miss Ross stood up and flung a glob home. It hit Papa right in the middle of the forehead.

Wiping his face, Papa shouted, "And good morning to the both of you!"

"Join us, Papa! We're getting mad!" I bent down to reload, then hit Miss Ross in the backside.

Miss Ross flung a handful of seeds at me, then shouted to Papa, "Bring your own fruit!"

Miss Ross and I were so busy flinging and shouting, we forgot about Papa. He showed up with a bucket of icy water. He stepped up behind me, then raised the bucket up over my head. I saw the water begin to pour and screamed as it hit my back. It was so cold, it stung. In a second, I was frozen right down to the pit of my stomach. I laughed, despite the cold.

Papa tipped the bucket back to save some water, then turned to Miss Ross. She'd seen him dump water on me, so she turned to run, but Papa caught up to her with one big stride and splashed her. She arched her back and screamed as the water hit her.

Miss Ross was so mad, she said she was ready to skin Papa alive. I was more than willing to help. I was still shivering as we ran after him. We didn't have any ammunition, so I wasn't sure what we'd do to him when we caught him. I wasn't even sure I could catch him. Papa was a good runner. Then Miss Ross threw herself at Papa and tackled him like a football player. I was so shocked, I just stood there watching as Papa rolled over and she started tickling him. Not even Mama would have tackled a man. Maybe Miss Ross wasn't the eternal flouncy-flossy I'd thought she was.

"Help me, Nissa," Miss Ross shouted, leaning on Papa to hold him down as she tickled him.

Papa shouted, "No, don't! I can't breathe!" The way he kicked and squirmed made Papa look as if he'd shrunk into a little boy.

"I'm going to get you, Papa!" I dropped to my knees. Miss Ross pulled back so I could tickle him.

"Ooh!" he shouted as he grabbed me by the waist and pulled me to the ground. Miss Ross came to my rescue and it felt pretty good. If I couldn't be with Mama, if I didn't have someone to teach me to dance, and paint, and read with a different voice for each character, then maybe, just maybe, it wouldn't be so horrible to spend time with a woman who enjoyed food fights and tickling fests.

I was sitting in a hot bath letting my thoughts drift around in the steam. Miss Ross had running water all through her house. There wasn't any pumping to be done and we didn't have to heat anything up to take a bath. I just turned the knob and, after a bit, steamy hot water came tumbling out. It was like a tiny little waterfall in the tub. Miss Ross even put in this liquid soap to make bubbles. I had gotten into the tub and it was like sitting in a hot lake with a cloud covering the surface of the water. I felt like Hera, queen of the Greek gods, looking down on Poseidon's water world.

As I sat there turning into a human pickle and looking at the shiny brass handles and the frilly towels, I thought about how Miss Ross could be my mama. If Papa had never met Mama, but married Miss Ross instead, I might've lived in a place like hers. What would it be like to have her as a mama, I wondered. I'd have to be careful not to mess up her pretty little things. I wondered what she thought of chasing butterflies, hoping she wouldn't catch them and stick them in a glass box. I couldn't imagine her playacting or making paper dolls. She probably preferred reading and piano lessons. She couldn't fly. Her feet were too heavy on the ground—she clomped when she walked. There was no float in her step. She'd probably be scared to sit on the roof of a porch. I already knew she was afraid of fires. But, she knew how to get mad. I wished Mama took her anger out on fruit instead of me and Papa.

I could feel a thought edging its way around my mind, then it snapped right into place so I had to pay attention. Mama had planned it. The whole thing. She'd walked out the door knowing Papa would never leave me without a mama. She'd decided she didn't want to be a mama anymore, so she'd gone. I wouldn't even put it past her to have picked Miss Ross out of a crowd as my new mama. I could see her slipping secret notes to Lara Ross about how special Papa was. I wasn't going to have it. No, sir. Mama wasn't going to run my life anymore.

Things were going to go my way. I wanted my own mama. The mama I was born to. My dedication to this new plan lasted only seconds. I didn't know where Mama was. She hadn't called. She hadn't written. There was no way to find her. Even her sister Sarah had no idea where she was. Mama had disappeared to let her little plan fall into place. I was stuck. I had to make the best of things.

Plunging under the water to rinse off my hair, I panicked. It was like drowning all over again for a split second. I gulped in water and came up coughing. Papa and Miss Ross called out together, "You all right, Nissa?" The sound of their voices in unison hung in my ears like the gong of a low bell.

"Fine," I shouted back, but the water didn't seem so cozy anymore and my idea about Mama's plan got kind of wobbly. As I got out to dry off, I decided I'd given Mama more than her due. She probably only knew Papa would take care of me no matter what. And there was a real small chance he'd made a pretty good choice by inviting Miss Ross into our lives.

Christmas

Each Christmas, Mama turned the house into a forest. She dug up baby cypress trees, planted them in big, old clay pots she'd painted red and green, then put them all over the house. She picked holly boughs and strung them up along the eaves and railings. Each time she bought a present, she put it in the biggest box she could find and wrapped it up in shiny paper. When she found just the right bow, she'd tie it and set the present in the first open spot she found. By December fifteenth, the house looked like a Christmas forest filled with cypress, holly, and the nearly extinct present bush!

The forest never grew that year. Grandma Dee was in charge of Christmas and she didn't do things Mama's way. She had Papa cut down a poor, defenseless fir tree. When I told him it was a sin to cut down a living thing, he said, "Well, I suppose this means you'll stop eating cows, vegetables, fruits, and eggs. I guess that leaves water."

I felt silly, but it didn't seem right to have a tree dying in our front room even if it did look all pretty decked out with ribbons and candy canes. Miss Ross and Grandma Dee worked for hours hanging those things on the branches, but it still looked like a dying tree to me. Grandma put all the presents under the tree and decorated the rest of the house with a bunch of candles. It looked like Christmas Eve service every night in our upstairs hall. Somehow it didn't seem so special after the fifth night, even with Miss Ross's silly idea of singing carols.

All I could think of was how much I missed Mama. I couldn't wait to get her letter. I knew she'd send one for Christmas like she did at Halloween. I was rushing to the post office every afternoon without even a second thought of old Chessie Roubidoux. Then the truth came out. I was helping Grandma Dee make her list for Christmas dinner. She was muttering about ham versus goose and I asked, "Is Grandpa Jared coming?"

"He's eating with Sarah and her family this year, Sweet Pea." She didn't even look up, she just kept on writing. Then I saw her make the *s* in *sauce* with an extra curlycue. I looked for the other letters. I'd read Mama's letter a thousand times. The paper was like silk after I opened and closed it and touched it so often. Sure enough, letter for letter, Grandma Dee's handwriting looked just like Mama's!

I ran upstairs. Unlocking Mama's desk, I searched for something she'd written. Anything. She tore up most of the things she wrote because she didn't like the way they looked. Finally, I found a note she'd written to herself. "Trim back the ivy before it eats us whole." It was tucked into a book on fertilizing your garden. I pulled out her letter. The *i*'s were the same, so were the *s*'s, but Mama crossed her *t*'s with a slant to the left and my letter had t-slants to the right. I ran back downstairs and stared at Grandma Dee's list.

"What's the matter with you, child?"

I stared at the *t*'s in *batter* and thought I'd scream. Grandma Dee's t-slants went to the right. "Here!" I slapped her stupid, lying letter on the table. "You can have this back!"

I ran out into the garden. Staring at the remains of Mama's flowers, the wilted blossoms and browning leaves made me realize just how Mama felt. She wanted things to live. She wanted them to be free and alive. I wanted to burn those dead things to the ground, make room for the new. I bent down and started to pull up the hibiscus, roots and all.

Papa came outside, asking, "What are you doing?"

"Why'd you bring her here? I want them to go away. Both of them."

He leaned down and took my hands in his. "Stop this now. Tell me what's going on."

"Grandma Dee sent that letter. Mama never sent me anything. She hates me and I hate her!" I pulled away from Papa and stood up.

"That's a lie," he said.

"So was that letter. You knew it, didn't you?"

Papa closed his eyes. I knew he couldn't lie about it anymore. I ran at him, my fists flying. He let me hit him, but I didn't feel any better. The letter was still a lie. Mama was still gone. I slumped down in his arms and he held me close, saying, "I'm sorry, Neesay. I didn't mean to hurt you. It was such a kind thing for Delia to try."

"It was mean."

"In the end, it was, but she only meant to help you."

"I want her to go away. Her and Miss Ross."

"You love your grandmother. You're just mad at her."

"And I'll stay mad."

"Really?" Papa lifted me up so we were looking at each other. "Even if I tickle you?" He tickled me and I couldn't help it. I felt loved and happy.

When we went back in the house, Grandma Dee wasn't in the kitchen. Miss Ross was there wrapping a present. "Where's Grandma Dee?" I asked.

"I think she went to her room."

Grandma Dee's room was the bedroom across from Mama's. We had a house big enough for a family of seven, but we'd never filled the other bedrooms. Maybe that's why Mama chose to have her own bedroom and Papa had a den—they wanted to fill the place up. Grandma Dee was sitting by the south window when I came in, her back to the door.

"Grandma Dee?"

She didn't answer me, so I went in. When I got up close, I saw that she was crying, her face red and puffy, her eyes blurry with tears. I wanted to hug her, but she held her hand up to keep me away.

"I did it because she should have. Your mother should have at least written you."

"I'm sorry I got so mad, Grandma." Seeing how much she hurt made me feel bad.

"Oh, I understand." She took my hand. "It was a foolish thing for me to do."

I put my forehead to hers. "I love you, Grandma Dee."

She hugged me. "Oh, don't you ever leave me, Nissa. I couldn't bear to lose you, too."

"Not a chance," I whispered.

* * *

Our Christmas wasn't quite right from the beginning and everything just got stranger as the actual day approached. Miss Ross was always popping in with another present to put under the tree. I kept thinking, doesn't she have a family of her own to send presents to? Grandma Dee was making enough sweets to feed every cicada in Louisiana and Papa was walking around talking to himself. I don't know what he was saying, but it must have been something good because he kept it up for over an hour one afternoon. The weather telegraphs from the news service were even talking snow!

The strangeness didn't end there. In fact, the snow they predicted came down as rain, and lots of it. The rain came down for thirty-six hours straight. The streets were big, long mud puddles by Christmas Eve. Miss Ross showed up with her skirt spattered with mud. Her and Grandma Dee were in the kitchen trying to wash it out. Papa was trying to keep water from washing up the bulbs in the flower bed. I was in the front hall skating through the water on the floor when there was a knock at the door. I figured it was someone else stuck in the road. I called for Papa, but he didn't hear me, so I answered it myself. It was a tall, black man hugging a big, balky tarp of some kind.

"This the Bergens'?" he asked.

I nodded. I stared at him a minute because I didn't know who he was, then he begged to come in out of the rain, so I invited him in. He went straight to the fire in the front room. Turned out, the tarp was his raincoat and he'd had it wrapped around a box that he set in front of the fire to dry.

"Who are you?"

"Will Thomas. Your daddy home?"

"He's in the garden."

"You go on and get him, now."

I wanted to stay and see what was in the box, but I ran back to get Papa.

"Who?" Papa asked, as I tried to shout through the rain.

"Come inside!" I yelled.

We stepped inside. Papa dropped his raincoat on the towel by the door, then followed me to the front room as I told him about the strange man. He was standing by the fire as Papa and I came in. He offered Papa his hand. "How do, sir. My name's Will Thomas. I was asked to deliver this package."

"By whom?" Papa asked as I knelt down by the box.

"A woman. She didn't give me her name."

I stared at the box. It had been covered with drawings that had run in the rain. It was from Mama. Only Mama could draw such wonderful flowers. "It's from Mama!" I shouted, tearing into the box. Papa tried to stop me, but I was already elbow deep in newspaper packing. Inside was a crystal angel. Around its neck was a note saying, "To watch over my baby Nissa." I was laughing and crying. It was really from Mama—the t-slants went to the left, the angel, the "baby." It was from Mama. She still loved me.

"Papa, look." I held it up and the light from the fire filled it with tiny flames.

"From Heirah."

"Who?" Will asked.

"Her mother." I didn't like the fact that Papa didn't say

his wife, but I was too happy with Mama's gift to care. I ran to show Grandma Dee. She laughed until she cried, too. I slept with that angel next to my bed that night and it hasn't been moved since.

Christmas morning, Miss Ross woke me up. Somehow, she got invited to our family Christmas. She pounced on my bed, saying, "Nissa, come down and open your presents."

"You want me to open my presents?"

"Yes, especially the ones I gave you."

"Don't you have a family of your own to go visit?"

"Nissa." Papa frowned from the doorway.

"Yes," Miss Ross nodded. "But the roads are washed out for miles around. Even the trains aren't coming in. You're stuck with me."

"Oh." I looked out the window. It was still raining and the sky was a dull gray. "What a Christmas."

Papa said, "It's what you make of it, Neesay. Now come on."

I got out of bed, then went downstairs. Half the presents under the tree were mine. Most of them were from Miss Ross. She bought me everything—a new dress, a pair of shoes, paints, even a book to write my thoughts down in. She bought pretty nice gifts. They weren't special, like Mama's, but they were nice. If Mama had given me a book to write my thoughts in, she would have written me a note inside and painted the cover with irises or clouds. The shoes would've had dried rose petals in them and the dress would have had cinnamon in the pockets. I held the plain, old, blue cotton dress up to my face wishing I smelled cinnamon and Miss Ross said, "I think she likes it."

"Do you like this?" Papa handed her a box. I knew from its size what it was. So did Miss Ross. Her fingers were just shaking to have that ring on her finger as she fumbled to get the tiny box open. Grandma Dee sat in her chair staring at the housecoat I gave her.

Papa finally had to open the box for Miss Ross. He pulled on the wrappping, saying "I've been practicing this moment for days, but it didn't do me any good."

That was why Papa was wandering around like a lunatic. If I'd a known, I would've interrupted. He popped open the box. The gold band inside looked so shiny, I wanted to throw it out in the rain. "Oh, Ivar," Miss Ross gasped.

"Do you like it?"

"It's beautiful." She pulled it out of the box and he slipped it on her finger. She gave Papa a big hug, saying, "Thank you, thank you."

"Does that mean the answer is yes?" Papa laughed.

"Yes. Oh, yes."

I was too shocked to move. I sat there staring as Papa planted his lips on that lady's mouth. I tried to remember the last time he'd kissed Mama on the lips. I recalled Papa coming into the kitchen just as Mama and I sat down to breakfast. He'd leaned over to give her a real kiss, but she'd turned her head and made it a peck on the cheek. That peck of a kiss made me think Mama might not love Papa in the right, married way. In fact, I knew it to be true and it made me cry.

Papa and Miss Ross saw me crying. Miss Ross held out her hand and said, "Come here, Nissa."

"Try to be happy for us, Neesay," Papa said, stroking my hair.

I hugged him with all my fear, my anger, and my sorrow. "I'm happy, Papa. I'm happy."

Marriage and Divorce

I WAS ALMOST CONVINCED HAVING MISS ROSS AROUND WOULDN'T be all that miserable. Then Mary and I went to Mr. Minkie's store that afternoon for some saltwater taffy. Mr. Minkie gets his taffy straight from New Orleans where they use the gulf water to make it good and salty.

We were fishing in the canister for blueberry. That's Mary's favorite. I was thinking of how it wouldn't be too hard to be without Mama if I had Papa, Mary Carroll, and Miss Ross; then I heard Mrs. Fisher talking to Mrs. Minkie back by the canned fruits. "It's bigamy. He should be arrested for even thinking of marrying another woman."

"Well, I heard he was never really married to Heirah in the first place. He wasn't even granted citizenship until last year." Mrs. Minkie talked as though she knew everything about my papa just by seeing him every Saturday.

I pulled my arm out of the canister, then tapped Mary to get her attention. I pointed at the women, saying, "They're talking about Papa." I knew I wouldn't have a minute of happiness if people in town didn't leave us alone. I sure didn't want to move into Miss Ross's place to get away from the townspeople. I wasn't about to give up any more of my old life. Mama was too much already.

Mary said, "I hope a big gust of wind knocks those peaches down on their heads."

"What's bigamy?"

"How should I know?"

"You knew about adultery."

"Does that mean I know every dirty word in the book?"

"Shh." I waved to quiet her so I could hear the women by the fruit.

Mrs. Minkie said, "Still, I think Lara Ross will be good for them. She's such a refined young woman, and stable. Ivar and Nissa need stability."

"If you ask me, you'd need to give her granite shoes to give that little girl stability."

I was angry. Mad enough to grab those jars of peaches and start throwing them myself. I wanted to knock those women silly, but I'd promised Miss Ross I wouldn't let my anger out in mean ways anymore. I clenched my fists and let the taffy squeeze out between my fingers.

Mr. Minkie must have seen me because he shuffled to the end of the counter. "Agnus," he called to his wife. "Help me get the flour down for these girls." He leaned his head toward Mary and me. The women turned as red as overripe watermelon when they saw us. We didn't even ask for flour, so I knew Mr. Minkie was just telling his wife we were there so she'd shut her mean, ugly trap.

I didn't want to hear another word. I had to get away from Mrs. Minkie and her gossipy friend, so I nudged Mary toward the door. Mr. Minkie wasn't as bad as his nosy wife, so I gave him a penny for the taffy I squashed, but I left the taffy. I didn't want his stinky candy.

Mary couldn't resist. She bought five pieces of blueberry taffy and put them all into her mouth at one time. Her lips were blue by the time we got to her house. "I've got to go in," Mary said, pointing to her front door.

Mrs. Carroll still wasn't real sure I wasn't the devil's child. She was a real nice lady, but she was a little mixed-up. I'd seen her shoo cats off the back steps because she thought they stole the breath of babies.

There were other people in town with the same ideas. In fact, half the town was convinced that Mr. Beauregard was really burying dead animals in his backyard after sacrificing their hearts to a voodoo god. Even Mrs. Owens put garlic on her back door on Halloween night to keep the evil spirits away. The people of Harper are beyond superstitious, they're just plain nuts. Especially Mrs. Carroll. Her devil-child idea was keeping Mary and me apart. We hadn't done anything more than go to Mr. Minkie's for taffy or cokes for the last two weeks and I knew for a fact that Mrs. Carroll watched us out of her bedroom window. I think she actually thought I could scoop Mary up and fly her away to secret, scary parts unknown.

Mary looked real sad about not being able to invite me in, but I shrugged and said, "It's all right." I wasn't happy about not being able to spend any real time with my best friend, but any complaints would be seen as evil, so I had to let Mary go inside without me. "See you later."

"Tomorrow. Maybe we can play tomorrow."

"Maybe."

I didn't look back as I walked home, but I'd bet a five-pound bag of licorice that Mary watched me all the way to my front porch. Her mom was strange, but Mary Carroll was tops.

Papa was on the porch when I got there, repainting the swing. Papa painted when he was happy, so I was glad to see him doing it even if he was painting slats the color of pine trees. "Morning, Nissa."

"Papa, what's bigamy?"

Papa wrinkled his brow. "Why do you and Mary talk about such things?"

"We didn't. I heard Mrs. Fisher say it in the mercantile."

"Were you eavesdropping?"

"She was practically shouting it. Besides, it's hard not to listen when you know someone's talking about your papa."

"It's better to turn the other cheek than to fill your head with the lies of gossip, Nissa."

"They said you weren't even married to Mama and that you were a bigamy."

He smiled as he shook his head. "I gather you're not willing to let this go."

"I can't stop thinking about it."

"Think of it this way—what you heard wasn't the truth."

"Well, I don't even know what it means."

"Nissa." Papa was warning me to stop pressing, but I had to know.

"Were you married to Mama?"

"Of course. On October 11, 1919. You know that."

"Tell me about the dance where you and Mama met."

"Your mama was there with one of the Journiette boys. I was there because I was working in the Journiette fields, picking cotton."

"And you met Mama and fell in love at first sight?"

"Not exactly."

"When did you fall in love?"

"Love doesn't just happen, Nissa."

"Do you love Lara Ross?"

Papa thought about it a moment, then said, "You don't always love the person you marry, Nissa. It starts with respect. The love will come."

"What about Mama. Didn't you love her?"

"Too much."

"You can't love someone too much."

He ruffled my hair. "Maybe not."

"You said you'd tell me about the dance."

He sat down, then leaned against the porch railing, still holding the brush in one hand. "Heirah was incredible," he said, thinking back. "I'd never seen a woman with such control of her body; she was like water contained in skin, she was so smooth and quick on her feet."

"Could she dance?" I asked, knowing she was the best dancer in Tucumsett Parish.

"She sure could. Everyone wanted to dance with her. She went from partner to partner."

"Did you ask her to dance?"

"Oh, no." He shook his head, smiling. "I was a bumble foot. I didn't want to embarrass myself."

"So she asked you?"

"Yes, ma'am. I was ladling out a cup of cider for myself

and your mother came up, flushed and out of breath."

"And pretty."

"She was sweating. Her dress was soaked through under the arms and wet around the open collar where it touched her chest. She was glistening. Her hair was sticking out of the braid and curling up around her face. What got me was her smile and the look in her eye. She was a mess and she didn't care because she was happy."

"She wasn't pretty?" Mama hated to sweat. It made her feel sticky and dirty. She thought she was prettiest after a nice hot bath. She said the steam even cleaned the inside of her skin.

"She was beautiful. She told me it was a sin to go to a dance and stand in the corner."

"So, you danced." I imagined them swirling onto the dance floor, everyone letting them pass as they stared into each other's eyes and fell in love. I thought it was just that simple. You looked at a man and knew he was the one you'd marry.

"Until I got blisters on my feet. Her escort had left hours earlier because she was dancing with so many other men, but she danced with me for hours."

"Because you were so handsome," I said, tweaking his chin.

He tweaked me on the nose. "No. She stayed with me because I talked to her. Most men asked her to dance, told her she was pretty, then never said another word. I talked to her."

"About what?"

"I have no idea. That was fourteen years ago."

"So you danced for hours and fell in love?"

"All right, I'll get to the love part." He leaned forward

and we rubbed noses. "Your mother asked me to walk her home. She was living with the Daytons and working in the old textile shop by the river."

"The one that burned down?"

"That's the one. We were on Miller Road. It was odd how blue everything looked in the moonlight, even our skin. She stopped at the Dayton place and sat on their fence. She stared at me for a second, then asked me to marry her."

"Just like that?"

"That's right. She said she'd never met a man who saw her as a person first and a woman second, so she didn't want me to get away."

"When did you fall in love?"

"I don't know exactly, but I was in the field when the smoke from the textile shop started billowing up on the horizon. I saw that smoke and panicked. I thought Heirah was dead and I just couldn't see myself without her. That's when I knew I loved her."

"But now you can live without her?"

He grabbed me and pulled me into his lap. Squeezing me, he yelled, "Neesay Marie! Why do you ask me all these impossible questions?"

"I'm curious."

"Too curious."

"But I've got to know."

"No you don't." He tickled me.

"Papa," I squealed.

He hugged me and I was about to ask him about what Mary said when I saw Mr. Ira Simmons walk on by again. He'd been doing it for months. Once a week, he'd waltz on by. For the life of me I couldn't guess what he was up to. He never stopped at the mercantile or said hello to anybody else to hide the fact he was walking by our place. He did come on different days and at all times of the day, but he always walked by once a week and gave our house a look. I watched him tip his hat like he always did, then looked at Papa.

Papa nodded to him, "Ira."

"Ivar."

I think they just like the way their names sounded, them being so similar and all. Papa saw me staring and tapped my chin. "Don't gawk, Nissa."

"Why's he always walking by?"

"Told me last week he was sizing up the place for when he builds his own. I invited him in, but he said he'd rather dream about what's inside."

Mama would like that answer, I thought. Maybe her and Mr. Simmons were just friends and that's why Miss Roubidoux saw them together. He probably missed Mama, too.

I thought about it for a moment, then realized Papa'd let Ira Simmons change the subject, so I asked, "What's bigamy?"

"Nissa!"

"Please?"

"Bigamy is being married to more than one person at the same time, but I won't commit bigamy, Nissa. Your mother and I will be divorced before I marry Lara."

"You'll divorce Mama?"

"In a way, she's already divorced me by leaving. I just have to make it official."

"How?"

"If you have to know, I put an ad in the paper that says I want to divorce your mother. If she doesn't answer the ad in three months, I'm free to marry Lara."

"Do you want Mama to answer it?"

"Don't ask me that, Nissa."

"Why not?"

"You won't like the answer." He stood up and went to the front door. "And neither will I."

After he went inside, I stood on the porch wondering just what answer I wouldn't like. If Mama came back, nothing would ever be the same. Papa would know she didn't love him, I'd know she'd wanted more children because I wasn't enough, and Mama would know Papa had courted Miss Ross. No one would be happy. Mama could stay away for all I cared. Miss Ross cared enough about Papa to ask him about Norway and worry when he was sad or tired. She also made Papa laugh. She'd make Papa a fine wife. That is, she would if she learned to make people-shaped muffins.

As for me, I didn't need her as a mama. I didn't need anyone at all. I'd done fine without mine for eight months' time. There was no need for another one.

Still, I couldn't help but look for Papa's ad. I had to read what he said to Mama when he knew she wasn't listening. I searched through the paper that Saturday. The ad was on the last page of the paper within a little black-line box that made it stand out. It read:

IVAR KNUT BERGEN OF HARPER, LA., ANNOUNCES HIS WILLINGNESS TO DIVORCE HEIRAH RAE BERGEN AS OF THIS DATE,

JANUARY 15TH, 1934. IF ANYONE SHOULD HAVE
ANY OBJECTIONS TO THE ABSOLUTION OF THEIR
WEDDING VOWS, PLEASE REPORT TO:
MR. ABBOT T. FIELDS,
ATTORNEY AT LAW,
16 WAKEFIELD ROAD,
HARPER, LA.
BY APRIL THE 15TH OF 1934.

The ad was so tiny, so clean and empty. The only thing
it really said was that Mama had three months to save her
marriage. It couldn't be done, but one corner of my heart
was still rooting for a miracle. I even clipped out the ad and
kept it in the sole of my shoe where every good girl kept a
nickel to call home. My nickel was in the other shoe.

Love and Friendship

NINETY DAYS. HOW LONG IS THAT EXACTLY? WHEN I'M IN school, time slows to the pace of sweat beading up on a cool day. I close my mind to the nasty comments about Papa stepping out with Miss Ross and focus on my schoolwork. I've never done so well in school in my life—can't say I'm proud of it, though. It's just a sign that I'm trapped in that stuffy schoolhouse where the days are divided into hours. Along about lunchtime those hours get broken down into minutes. Right before the bell rings for dismissal those minutes are chiseled into seconds.

Time's different on the weekends. I get up in the morning and hit the floor ready to run right through to the end of the day. I go straight to the Carrolls' on most weekends. I give Mrs. Carroll a sweet from Grandma Dee's big supply as a peace offering, then Mary and I go out to the creek to hunt up grubs to sell at a penny a pound to Mr. Minkie. Grub hunting's best when the ground is still wet from the dew and the sun's still hiding behind the clouds. Our problem is we get to hunting up newty lizards and talking so much the sun's up and burning our hides before we find a fistful of grubs. No sooner have we covered the bottoms of our buckets with the slimy, squirmy moneymaking grubs, than Mrs. Carroll's voice comes drifting down off the bluff over the creek, calling Mary back when she has the noon meal on the table. We take the grubs to Mr. Minkie, then go our separate ways. I'm too hungry to think about what I'm eating and lunch is over before I'm real sure it began. The afternoons disappear into a nap on a garden bench or a game of Twenty Questions with Grandma Dee. Then it's jacks on the Carrolls' front porch until dinner.

On Sunday nights, after Grandma gets back from calling Grandpa Jared, I help her work on my dress for Papa's wedding. We sit at the end of the porch closest to the Carrolls' house. While we're working, I sometimes hear April reading to her brothers and sister. Each time I hear her high-pitched reading voice chopping through sentences, I pray she doesn't start reading about Pooh Bear and his friends. It'd make me cry to hear anyone but Mama read about how Pooh got his head stuck in a honey pot and Piglet feared heffalumps.

Most times I try to keep my mind on nothing but the needle and thread in my hand. I stare at the dirt behind my nails as I baste the stitches, then Grandma Dee makes them secure and neat. If I wasn't so crumpled up inside, I might've thought the dress Grandma Dee was making looked pretty. It was yellow—the color of the sun in the picture book about the elephant who got lost among redwood trees when he escaped from a zoo. Even if I am too old for them, I'd rather have another one of those picture books than a dress for Papa's wedding. I could sit in the back of the church and read it instead of sitting up front with Miss Ross's family.

If it was the evening Ira Simmons chose to walk by and look at our house, we'd all wave and say, "Good evening." He'd reply and disappear into the dark. He'd get me to thinking about sawdust and wondering where Mama was. I'd poke myself with the needle and have to start forgetting everything all over again.

Papa and Miss Ross spent their evenings admiring each other with silly little whispers as they rocked away on the porch swing. In my mind, I just make them disappear along with April and the buzzy bugs all around and even Mama, I guess. I make everything disappear so there's nothing but me, a needle, thread, and a stupid old dress I never want to wear.

Ninety days can pass quicker than a flash flood when you forget to look at a calendar for days at a time and keep track of the days by the events within them. Tuesday was the day April bet Mary a nickel that she wouldn't eat a grub. Wednesday was the day Mary used her nickel to buy a handful of blueberry taffy. Saturday was the day Miss Ross got her heel stuck between the slats of the front porch and had to use a jackknife to pry her shoe out. The days melted into weeks and it was the fifteenth of April before I had the time to really decide how I felt about divorce.

Mary said divorce was against the sacrament of marriage and people went to hell for breaking a sacrament. All I can say to that is Catholics sure do spend a lot of time worrying about hell. In my mind, God loves us all, so there's no way He's sending someone He loves to hell just because they break His rules.

When I thought about God's love for a while, I figured that explained why I still loved my mama. I could spit fire when I recalled her leaving me without saying good-bye. I cried every time I thought about the fact that she wouldn't have even been at my funeral if I'd drowned for good in the river. All that said and done, I still loved my mama. God's love helped me love Mama. He showed me how to love without a memory of bad things. Truth was, I missed her so awful bad I still slept with her pillow.

I went to bed at night hugging her pillow tight to draw in Mama's vinegary smell, praying I'd dream of her like Grandma Dee said I might. Occasionally, I did. She'd be standing in the distance with her back to me, no shoes on her feet, but a straw hat on her head. She'd be carrying her suitcase in one hand and hailing a bus with the other. Some nights I wanted to take that bus with her; other nights, I threw rocks at the windows. But mostly I walked home alone and Papa was there at the gate to meet me.

All that time, all those thoughts and dreams and I still didn't know what I really felt about Mama. Of course, I knew I loved her, but I didn't really know where to put her in my heart. Having Grandma Dee around didn't help much. Papa said she stayed to help me adjust, but she packed away all of Mama's things and put them in the attic. She said she did it to keep Mama's things safe, but I knew she never expected to see Mama again. You don't pack people's things away unless they're dead or gone forever, like Baby Benjamin.

I watched Grandma Dee folding Mama's clothes. She

didn't fold them over her arm like she did when she took the clothes off the line. She laid them out on the floor, ran her hand over the fabric like she was smoothing the ripples on water, then gently picked up a sleeve or a skirt hem with her fingertips to fold it. She straightened every collar and buttoned every button. She worked with such quiet care it was as if Mama were inside each piece of clothing and Grandma Dee was tucking her away to keep her safe and warm in the attic.

Was Mama really safe? Even if he loved her, was the Sawdust Man good to Mama? Did he keep her safe from harm? Mama said there are some men who think it's all right to hit a woman. Mama would hit him back, I'm sure of that, but did he have enough money to buy her warm food and clothes? I prayed he didn't take her up North where the cold air freezes into snow.

All my worrying didn't help much. It made my mama into a shivering image in my mind that I could take down and store away like Grandma had done with her things. Late at night, when I couldn't sleep, I'd imagine myself walking up the creaky stairs to the attic and opening the door to find Mama in her beautiful violet gauzy dress, the moonlight from the window shining through it and making Mama look as though she were glowing. She'd be unpacking all her things and smiling at how careful Grandma Dee had been about packing them. She'd turn to say, "She kept them safe for me, Nissa. Nice and safe."

I'd say, "Who kept *you* safe, Mama?"

She'd smile even bigger and say, "The Lord."

Her voice would be so soft and musical, I was sure she

was an angel now. Sometimes I thought that whole vision was just God's way of saying she was dead. I thought maybe God had told Grandma Dee Mama was dead and that's why she packed away all of Mama's things. When I got to thinking about Mama dying, I couldn't do anything but cry.

It was all silly I suppose. There was no way of knowing what had really happened. No one to ask. No one to tell. Mama was lost to the world and everyone in it except herself and the stinking old Sawdust Man. It'd serve her right if Papa got married to somebody else. She'd left it so no one could even so much as give her a proper burial. Papa didn't owe her anything. He was free to marry Miss Lara Ross.

But Grandma Dee didn't think so. I caught her mumbling to herself about the wedding as she was washing Mama's canning jars, ready to put up the cherry preserves. She was staring out the window, dunking a jar up and down in the soapy water and whispering, "Walking around like she owns the place."

"What's that, Grandma?" I pulled a chair up to the sink so I could see out the window.

Grandma Dee pointed at Miss Ross who was pruning the azaleas. "Look at her acting like *she* planted them."

I was hoping the clippers would slip and she'd snip off some of her sleeve, or perhaps a bit of her silly leather gardening gloves. Putting a little gravel in my voice, I said, "I told her I'd cut back the bushes myself."

"They're your mother's flowers," Grandma Dee told me. "We should leave them until they grow into an ugly tangle. Then Heirah would know she can't just walk away." Grandma Dee wasn't saying those things to me really. She was wiping the same jar over and over again as she talked, her eyes fixed on Miss Ross.

I'm not sure if she was speaking to anyone in particular, or even listening to what she was saying; she was just talking. "That's the problem. When she got fed up with the flowers she was grooming for the fair, she'd just chop them all to pieces, then storm off. Her father would go out there, save what blossoms could be salvaged, and she'd get a white ribbon. It happened every year.

"If her father had left those flowers, Heirah would have lost her ribbon and maybe, just maybe, she would have had more patience the next year. Ivar was just the same as her father. The patience of Job, the love of John the Baptist." She nodded without looking at me. I didn't want her to stop. I wanted her to say everything that came to mind. If I reminded her I was there, she would've stopped herself, then picked only the things she thought a child should hear. It was much better to remain an invisible, ageless listener.

"When she tried to run off the first time and destroyed her beautiful garden, Ivar went all the way to Chicago to buy those stupid purple roses. If he made her clean up after her own temper tantrums, maybe she'd still be here—instead of that stupid, husband-stealing woman." She shook a jar at Miss Ross.

I agreed with Grandma Dee, but it didn't matter what we thought. Mama had left and there was nothing Papa or I could do to change that. Papa had asked Miss Ross to marry him and Grandma Dee couldn't stop them. Still, there were a lot of people against the whole idea of Papa getting remarried.

* * *

Usually everyone in town was talking about the next wedding and offering food, advice, and an endless number of services, from sewing bridal gowns to mowing the lawn before the reception. For Papa's wedding there were no such offers. Few people even spoke about the wedding above a whisper. I'd heard Miss Chessie Roubidoux and Mrs. Dayton twittering over by the fabric in the mercantile and overheard Papa's name in quiet whispers in the foyer of the church after services, but no one so much as offered a snarling congratulations when Miss Ross brought a rhubarb-strawberry pie to the church bake-off and I'm sure it's not just because she won first prize. Not that it was really worth my time to wonder, but I couldn't figure out why people were so cold about Papa's wedding. Then April Carroll set me straight.

She cut my hair the day before the wedding and, as they say, "filled me in." April's parents didn't think it was right for their children to go to the wedding on account of their view of divorce and remarriage as sin, but Mrs. Carroll didn't see anything wrong with April cutting my hair for the occasion. I needed my hair cut regardless of what I did afterward.

"Nissa, you know why no one in this place has lifted a finger for Miss Ross?" April asked me as she snipped away.

"No." I never talked much when April was cutting my hair. She always cut it crooked if I moved around a lot and I can't talk at all without moving my head or my arms. Besides, *she* did so much talking it wouldn't have done me any good to try and interrupt.

"Well, besides the fact that there are brainless plugs like

my brother Teddy and his pal Peter Roubidoux who go around saying Miss Ross used a voodoo love brew on your pa."

I felt my body get all tough and prickly. That Peter Roubidoux had manure for a heart. My papa wouldn't fall prey to any voodoo brew.

"Sit still before I cut off an ear."

"Sorry."

"You see, people just have bad ideas about Miss Ross. I even wiggle my ring finger during mass and half the congregation is ready to sew my gown, but Lara Ross had to send to New Orleans for hers. I'll tell you why, too. Me, I'm young. I'm supposed to marry a young gentleman and settle down to start a family. Miss Ross lost her chance when she was still young. Now, she's what people call a man-hunter, the type of woman who would do anything for a husband. She didn't marry Bobby Journiette when she had the chance, so now she'll take lives to have a family."

I thought to tell her that Papa was the one who'd offered to help Miss Ross out of her car, invited her for a picnic, and asked her to marry him, but I realized it was useless because April had a rhythm going—cut a little, then gossip; cut a little, gossip. She wasn't even stopping to take a breath. I only hoped she didn't scalp me before she was through talking.

"Well, everyone is convinced that good old Lara scared your ma off so she could have a crack at your pa."

"Piss and vinegar!" I shouted. I'd reached my boiling point and was ready to spew steam. "There's no way in this world anyone could scare my mama off. Folks are just hunting for stories. If the people in this town saw a donkey in a tree, they'd guess it'd sprouted wings!"

Love and Friendship 213

April laughed. "Sometimes you can be the perfect copy of your mama."

"Darn straight! Mama isn't afraid of anything." Especially not some glove-wearing woman.

"You got that right."

I smiled, but I wasn't happy inside. The smile on April's face said it was a good thing to be the daughter of Heirah Rae Bergen. Only, Mama wasn't a Bergen anymore. It was Lara Ross's turn to be Papa's wife.

Not that he'd bothered to ask before he proposed to her, but Papa suddenly got worried that I might be upset about him getting married. When I came back from the Carrolls' that afternoon, he called to me from his study. When Papa had a "clean your room" or "don't forget your homework" thing to say, he'd just wait until we met up somewhere and say it. But when he had to ask me a "How would you feel about going away to a private school" sort of question, he found me or called me to him. Now, if it was something spectacular, like Mama was coming home and he was packing Miss Ross off to Canada or something, he'd run to find me, yelling my name all the way. Knowing his habits like I do, it wasn't hard to guess he was calling me to ask how I felt about the wedding. It didn't matter what I thought anymore, so I kept right on going.

Truth was, I was on a mission. I went up to Mama's room. I wanted to find the key she kept under the bottom dresser drawer so I could lock the door. I didn't want sappy old Miss Ross moving in. I'd take Mama's room before I'd let anybody else in there. I couldn't take seeing anybody but

Mama floating by the open windows. I stood there remembering the way she looked, waltzing by the folded shutters, her bare feet soundless, the folds of her violet dress trailing behind her like a fog.

I found the key, but I couldn't lock the door. It was too much like shutting Mama away in the past—saying she'd never be back. I went to her closet instead. I opened the door. The smell of cedar and dust drifted out of the empty space. Grandma had already put Mama away. Seeing that closet bare as a dead tree hollowed me out. I was crying by the time I reached the attic door.

It was hot enough to make my eyeballs sweat up there, but I had to find Mama's dancing dress. I had to put it against my skin, smell her scent in the fabric, know she wasn't so far away I couldn't have a little piece of her to keep.

I wanted Mama to know how careful Grandma Dee had been, so I took everything out of the box a piece at a time. I pulled out the skirt of my dress to lay them on so they didn't get dusty. I could hear Papa calling me as I worked, but I had to find Mama's violet dress. I unpacked and repacked three boxes before I found it. The gauzy fabric was cool to the touch even in that nasty heat. Under the folds of see-through fabric was a silky underpart that went against the skin. Mama's skin. It smelled of Mama and the night air. I ignored the dusty smell of the attic and thought of Mama twirling in the music of a fiddle.

"Nissa." Papa had only whispered, but I nearly jumped to the rafters.

I put the dress in my lap as Papa weaved his way through the boxes. "Look at these boxes." He put his hand on Mama's baby-pink shirt with the swan-shaped patch on the shoulder. "Dee put these away as if she was packing priceless china."

Leave it to Papa to be where Mama should be. I wanted to see Mama in the attic admiring Grandma Dee's care, knowing the love it showed, but it was Papa standing there smiling over those boxes. I hated him for it and I loved him for it. No, I hated Mama for not being there and loved Papa for never leaving.

Papa sat on Mama's steamer trunk. "Mama ever tell you about that dress?" He nodded at my lap.

I rubbed the dress. "No."

"It came straight from Oslo."

"Really?" I imagined it hanging in a window with snow piled up on its ledges and people milling by in sweaters knitted in yarns of a hundred different colors, ice-topped mountain peaks poking over their heads in the background.

"My Uncle Erling sent it to us."

"The one who eats the stinky cheese?"

"Yes, he eats limburger cheese from Germany."

"And smells like he's sucked on raw fish."

Papa laughed. "He did when I was three."

"He sent this to Mama?"

"For our wedding day."

"It's purple!"

Papa chuckled. "Yes, well the other thing you should know about Uncle Erling is that his eyes are kind of cloudy and he doesn't see colors quite right. He thought it was white."

I laughed. Papa added, "Heirah thought it was fantastic.

She said God showed Erling which dress to pick. God knew she loved the color purple."

It was too funny to think of God helping somebody shop, but it made my fingers tingle to know I was holding Mama's wedding dress. "Mama was married in this dress?"

Papa slid down onto the floor next to me and touched the dress. Holding out the skirt, he said, "Yes, ma'am. And she was beautiful."

As Papa held the skirt up, I could see the jagged edges of the tear down the back. "How'd that happen, Papa?"

Papa frowned, then hummed to himself a bit. "That happened on our fourth anniversary."

"Tell me about it, Papa."

He put his arms out behind him and leaned back. I could see his eyes drifting back in time with his memory. I know he was reseeing that night and I wished I could be there with him. "We always danced with all the windows opened, even if it rained."

"In her room, like Mama and me?"

"All over the house. We were dancing in the garden when it happened. The Charleston, I think. Heirah's dress got caught on a rosebush and, quick as a wing beat, it was ripped. Your mama cried all night over that rip. She sat right down on the wet flagstones and cried. She didn't even come in when lightning struck the Daytons' crab apple tree across the way. I had to carry her in to bed."

"Why'd she cry so much, Papa?" Her dress was special, but not worth crying all night over—even if you couldn't sew the rip on account of the fabric being so delicate.

He sighed. "I can only guess, but I think she thought it

meant we wouldn't stay together. She thought a rip in her wedding dress meant our marriage wouldn't last."

"She was right."

"Nissa, we were married for ten years after that. The end of our marriage has nothing to do with a rip in a dress."

Papa was right, but I wanted to know the real reasons their marriage ended. How could people who danced in the rain not stay in love? I asked, "So what did end it?"

He took the handkerchief out of his pocket and wiped the sweat off my chin, then handed it to me to wipe the rest of my face. "Nissa, do you understand how airplanes fly or know what God really looks like?"

I tried to think about the questions, but my mind was instantly muddled with partial images of plane wings and angels floating over clouds. "Why'd you ask me those things?"

"Because, Nissa, you want to know everything. You need a reason for everything. I don't doubt there's a reason and an answer for each little thing in this world, but you aren't ready for them all." He tapped my head. "No one is. And sometimes you ask me things little girls just shouldn't even think about."

"Little girls shouldn't think about love and marriage?"

"Love, yes. Marriage, no. That's why girls wait to become women before they take a husband."

I was mad at Papa for treating me like a child, so I said, "You just don't know the answer."

Papa pulled my braid. "Don't be spiteful. I didn't tell you because you don't need to know. Be happy knowing that your papa loves you." He kissed me on the ear. "Your mama loves you." He bit my earlobe and made me squeal.

"Your nana loves you." He gave me a big hug like Grandma Dee would, then got up. "And Lara loves you." He tapped my shoulder.

"She does?"

"Sure. No one cries for someone they don't love."

"She cried for me?" I asked.

"When you threw yourself in the river, she drove us to the hospital. She cried all the way there."

"For you. I hit you." I cringed with the memory of the awful bruises I put on Papa's face.

"For you." He tapped my nose. "All the way there she was saying, 'God please don't take this little girl.'" Papa was smiling, but his eyes were all teary.

It was only for an instant, but I felt my heart go warm. Miss Lara Ross loved me. That was a wicked thought. I couldn't love her. She wasn't my mama. No way. She'd marry my papa, but she'd never be anything more than Miss Ross to me. Heavens, I thought. She wouldn't be Miss Ross much longer. She would be marrying Papa in a short while. That meant I couldn't call her Miss Ross anymore. Damned if I was going to call her mama, but calling somebody Mrs. Bergen just didn't sound right.

I finally figured it'd be all right to call her Lara. After all, she'd said a while back that she wanted me and her to be friends. I still didn't think that was possible, but her idea solved my name problem, at least. Then again, it isn't proper to talk to a grown-up using their calling name. It's only proper if you call them Mr. or Mrs., Miss or Uncle or Aunt or some such title. Mama always laughed when people called her Mrs. Bergen. She thought it made it sound like she should have a pile of hair in a tight old bun on her head and wear stiff white shirtwaists with a brooch at the collar. Miss Ross made me think of snobby old gloves and clicky heels that catch in porch boards. Lara made me think of a woman driving to a hospital and asking God to save a child's life. I could call her Lara. The only trouble was—would she let me?

I didn't work up the starch to ask Miss Ross what I was supposed to call her until the next morning. I went into the guest bedroom across from Mama's where she was getting ready. Her dress was white with all sorts of frilly bows and stiff creases. She was nothing like Mama.

"You mind if I call you Lara?" I asked Miss Ross as she put her earrings on. She was shaking on account of the fact the wedding was only half an hour away.

Miss Ross closed her eyes, then looked at me with a smile on her face, saying, "I'd like that Nissa, thank you."

I didn't expect her to thank me. I felt kind of embarrassed. She picked up her hairbrush and tried to use it backward.

"Nervous?" I asked, taking the brush, then going behind her to help her with her hair.

"Yes."

"I've never been in a wedding either."

She turned and took my hand. "Nissa, are you sure you're not angry with us for getting married? I wouldn't do this if I knew it was hurting you."

I answered her from my gut. My head and my heart had nothing to do with it. "If Mama can have her Sawdust Man, then Papa deserves you."

Miss Ross blinked. "Heavens. Well, I guess I'll take that as your blessing."

"If you like."

"Nissa!" Grandma Dee's voice boomed through the house like a train horn.

I ran out into the hall yelling, "Yes, ma'am?"

"Come down here so I can put your dress on."

I ran down to the front hall. Shucking the daisy-print dress Mama made me last year, I threw up my arms to let Grandma Dee slide the dress over me. She stood there in front of the hall mirror with her hands behind her back like she was hiding a Christmas present. "Your papa and I got to talking last night, so I made you a little surprise."

"Surprise?" What more could she add? My dress already had pearly buttons with pink petals sewn around them. Just the night before I'd seen her putting the butter-yellow ribbon on the inside of the hem to finish it off like they do in department stores.

"Just close your eyes and I'll put it on you."

I closed my eyes and felt a silky fabric slide over me. My eyes popped open and I was staring at a stranger in the mirror. There was an ugly little girl in a pretty purple dress. Mama's dress was on me! Grandma had cut away the bottom of the silky skirt and the nasty rip with it. She even found a way to flip the gauzy skirt up to attach the bottom hem to the waist. "Grandma Dee," I gasped.

She stepped back. "Aren't you just the picture of your mama."

No, I wasn't. I was wide and pudgy where Mama was thin and narrow. My feet were soft and pink while Mama's were hard and tan. I looked like a twisted old troll in a ball gown. I wiggled and shook until I was out of that dress and ran for it. I couldn't believe Grandma Dee had ruined Mama's wedding dress only to put ugly old me inside. I was out the back gate and running for Mary's house before I knew what I was doing.

Mrs. Carroll came charging at me from her clothesline with a sheet in her hand. "Cover yourself, child!" She threw the sheet over my shoulders and herded me to the house.

I would have said something, but I was a hornet's nest of emotions—feeling a thousand things at once. My head was buzzing. Mrs. Carroll sat me down on their back porch. "What happened, Nissa?"

I looked past her at the back door. She was the last person I wanted to speak to. She thought I was the devil's child. "Where's Mary?" I asked.

"Gone with her father to get new church clothes. Now tell me what happened."

"I'll go home."

"Not in my sheet, you won't. You tell me what happened and I'll go and get a dress of Mary's."

Mary said when Catholics sin, they have to pay a penance. It's like working off the price of a window when you throw a baseball through it. If you do something wrong, you have to do something nice to erase the bad thing you did. I figured telling Mrs. Carroll was the only way I could make up for running through the neighborhood like a midgety Lady Godiva in only my underpants and without a horse.

To get it over with quickly, I flat out said, "Grandma Dee ruined Mama's dress and tried to make me wear it to

Papa's wedding." It seemed easy enough to stop when I started, but I just kept on going. It was like I'd put too much coal into my fire and there was no putting on the brakes. "Can you imagine that? Chopping up your own daughter's wedding dress so you could put it on your granddaughter for the wedding of your son-in-law to some lady you don't even like?"

Mrs. Carroll did something I'd never seen her do before. She laughed. I've seen her crack a smile and chuckle a little, but she let out a shake-the-plates chortle and turned red in the face as I sat there with my mouth hanging open.

Finally, she caught her breath and said, "Child. Dear child." She put her hand on my knee and gave it a little squeeze. "You ever wonder why I try to put the Red Sea between you and Mary when I know full well you two will be best friends until your dying days?"

"No." I couldn't believe she was actually admitting to doing such a thing. I suppose it was an eye-for-an-eye kind of trade. I told her a truth, she told me one. It seemed like a pretty nice idea to me. I even so much as thought I might run into Mrs. Carroll's yard half naked more often.

"Well, I remember the first time I saw you. You were in the garden with your mother. I came over with some iced tea and cookies—a welcome gift."

I could see her coming through the back gate in a long dress that swaggered when she walked. It had big sunflowers on it and I thought they were smiling at me. "I remember that."

"I'm sure you do." She said it in an "I agree, but don't approve" sort of way and I started to get nervous. "You and your mother were sitting on the flagstones sorting seeds."

"Yes." I nodded. I didn't care what Mrs. Patricia Carroll thought. I loved that afternoon. Mama and I were facing each other, our toes touching. We were counting seeds so Mama could replant the garden after she'd burned it down. Mama'd say, "Here's poppy seeds, Nissa. You show Mama five poppy seeds."

I'd count them out real slow: one, two, three, four, five. I usually forgot the four though. When I got it right, Mama would squeal, "Goodie-goodie-go-go-girl!" We'd wiggle our toes together and laugh.

I scrunched my toes as Mrs. Carroll kept talking. "You were just a little pip. Barely three years old and you were counting past ten and sorting out seeds by their kind. You flat out told me your mother burned the garden to make the soil better for the baby plants to grow."

"Is that bad or something?" I was getting angry, but I was also sitting on a front porch in a sheet, so I kept my tongue.

"Not really, Nissa, but I think you were already five years old when you were born. Every time you have a birthday, you grow five years older."

I wondered if she and Miss Ross had been talking about me dealing with "adult issues." I wanted to say if they were so worried about me growing up too fast, then why didn't they keep their poky noses out of my life, but to be respectful, I said, "That'd make me nearly sixty years old!" Once again, I'd proved I wasn't Mama's daughter. She still counted on her fingers and toes. She'd stand on the front porch pointing down at her feet tallying up the change she should've gotten. Mrs. Minkie often shortchanged her and she'd have to march on back for her proper change.

Mrs. Carroll shook her head. "Sixty sounds about right. Nissa, you've got your father's thinking cap, your mother's deep well of emotion, and a hundred years of living in a ten-year-old's body."

"I'm eleven, almost twelve."

"That's not the point, Nissa. You're too old for your age and I don't want my Mary missing out on her childhood. I want to let her grow up slow and natural without all those deep thoughts that keep you brooding and running around half naked."

I laughed. Mrs. Carroll tried not to, but I saw her lips screw into a smile. If she was so worried about Mary growing up slow, she should keep her away from April. If I was sixty, April was 170. "I won't do anything to Mary, Mrs. Carroll."

"I know that." Mrs. Carroll touched her chest. "My heart knows that. Now if only I can convince my head."

I forced a smile. She tapped my knee. "I better get you home. I'll go get a dress."

She went inside. I started to look around her yard thinking how weird it was to actually talk to Mrs. Carroll. I thought maybe she never talked to me because she thought I was smarter than she was. Nah. An adult wouldn't be thinking things like that. I was about ready to go inside and help Mrs. Carroll when I saw Grandma Dee standing at the post marking the end of the Carrolls' yard. She was holding the yellow dress. When she saw me, she held it out.

I wanted to run to her and put the dress on and I wanted

to melt into the side of the house. I was always going crazy—running into rivers, throwing roses, running around the neighborhood like a lunatic—I'd probably never make it to sixty. I stood up and opened the screen door, slow as you please. "Thank you, Mrs. Carroll, but Grandma Dee is here with a dress."

"Oh." Mrs. Carroll sounded kind of dazed as she came to the door. She held up a hand to wave to Grandma Dee who was crossing the yard, but she let it drop, then went into the kitchen instead.

She was leaving the two of us alone, so it was time for me to face Grandma Dee. I turned around. Grandma Dee was slouched and teary eyed. Funny thing, though, I didn't feel bad. I felt even. She'd cut up Mama's wedding dress. I'd almost made her cry. Sounds awful, but that's the way I felt.

"Sorry, Grandma." I didn't want her to feel bad anymore.

"Your papa told me how much you loved that dress. I didn't know Heirah was married in it."

Papa must have told her, but I wanted to know why she didn't know in the first place. "You weren't at the wedding?"

"I had no idea she was even married until she and Ivar showed up on our doorstep for Christmas." It finally struck me. Mama and Grandma Dee weren't like Mama and me. We were friends. We talked. We played. We danced. They'd probably never danced together in their lives. We never saw Grandma Dee and Grandpa Jared but once or twice a year and they only lived an hour or two away by train. They didn't even hug when they met. Mama just kissed Grandma Dee on the nose like she did when Papa was shaving. When they made meals together, they'd stand back-to-back, never saying more than two words at a time. I used to think it was because they knew each other's thoughts, but now I know it's because they never really talked. They probably didn't know what to say to each other.

I knew what I'd say to Mama if she was there right then. "How dare you? We shared almost everything in the world, then you left. I can't forgive you for that. Go away."

For the first time, I felt like I didn't want to see Mama again. Friends don't walk out on each other—especially not mother-friends. It was like Mrs. Carroll said, "Friends should be together until their dying days." Papa would do that. He'd live an extra hundred years just so he could be there to make sure I wasn't afraid to die.

Oh sassafras. Mrs. Carroll was right. Such thoughts didn't belong in my head. What was I doing thinking about death on a wedding day? In the turn of a knob, I was ready to put on the yellow dress Grandma held out to me and walk right into that church pretty as a sunflower and give my papa away to Miss Lara Ross.

A Miracle

I sat in the front pew watching Papa face Miss Ross, the preacher saying the marrying words, and all my anger just floated away. I didn't hate Mama. I hated the fact that she was gone and the wedding meant she'd never come back. I started wishing for a miracle that could wash away everything and bring Mama back. Oh, I was sick of wishing, so tired of thinking.

As if God heard me lose hope, it started to rain. I didn't notice it for a while, then a thundercloud rumbled. Grandma Dee always said thunder meant God was clearing His throat to get people's attention. I started listening to the rain pelting the tin roof and sat up with a smile. Maybe God would grant me a miracle after all.

All of Lara's happy relatives shaking hands and laughing didn't faze me any. I floated home among the people who were going back to the house to celebrate the wedding. I stood by the back door where I could see all the people milling in and out of the rooms. I'd see the surprise on their faces when Mama came through the door. Everyone would stop. Mama'd have on that tiny slip of a smile that made men nervous. Papa would come out into the hall with Lara who'd start to shake.

Mama would rattle the newspaper with the divorce notice in Papa's face saying you can't divorce nobody through a newspaper and declare his marriage stupid and unlawful. Miss Ross would run away crying. All her relatives would follow. Mama and Papa would fight until dawn in Papa's study and things would get back to normal in a few weeks.

As the hours went by, I realized what a fool I'd been believing in such a fairy tale. God isn't a fairy godmother and He doesn't make custom-fit miracles. Like Mama always said, "God answers all your prayers, but He gives you what you need, not what you ask for."

Did that mean I needed to be without Mama? That thought made me feel sick. Looking for a way to make my stomach stop whirling, I found a bowl brimming full of butter mints. I ate them until they coated my mouth, hoping I'd explode.

There were people everywhere. Miss Ross had enough relatives to fill our house. I wish they'd all disappear in puffs of smoke. It rained all afternoon and they were still all cheery—drinking, eating, shouting. They were pinching and patting me as if I was a dog, so I sat under the hall table, watching happy feet shuffle by and eating my mints. Papa found me there hugging the empty bowl.

"Nissa, how many of those have you eaten?" He took the bowl away from me and wiped my face with his napkin.

"A few," I muttered.

"You look absolutely green."

"Hmmm."

"What is it, Nissa?"

"I'm fine," I said.

"You're fine? I'm President Roosevelt."

"I'm tired."

"Tell me the whole truth now, Nissa. What is it?" Papa actually crawled under the table with me. The back of his head was pressed against the tabletop and his neck looked almost broken, but he was there, waiting and listening.

"She's never coming back."

Papa pinched me hard on the thigh.

"Ouch!"

"That's for doubting your mother's love for you." He looked at me from the corner of his eye. "If I know Heirah and, believe me, I do, the only reason she's been gone this long is because she's afraid you'll be too mad to let her back into your life."

"I wouldn't do that." I never told him what I thought in the Carrolls' backyard and I cursed myself for thinking it.

"She would if you and I walked out on her." He raised his eyebrows.

"She would?"

"That's right and she's awful worried that you're just like her."

"She is?"

"She always said that." Papa held his breath for a second. He did that when he was about to say something he probably shouldn't. "She used to say, 'Ivar, what if our girl is as selfish and unforgiving as I am?'" He looked at me, his eyes wide.

I thought about it. He was right. Mama was selfish. She did what Mama wanted—burned her garden despite the threat to the house, decided to go to dance school, and left with another man. Plus, she still won't buy so much as a penny stamp from Chessie Roubidoux for slapping her in the face.

"I'm not like her."

"Come here." Papa took me by the hand and led me upstairs. We went into his room. I never went in there. He didn't lock the door or anything. It just didn't seem right to go into Papa's room. A part of Papa is quiet and separate. I think I'd call it his privacy. And it didn't seem right to go in Papa's private places.

Walking in, I wondered where Mama's private place was? We were almost always together. Where'd she go to be alone? I was free to walk right into her room without knocking. Anybody could waltz right through her garden or the kitchen. I never even knew her to lock the bathroom door when she took a bath.

It wasn't like Papa didn't share with me. He just didn't share everything. He kept part of himself private and whole for just him and God to share. That'd be pretty nice, especially if it wasn't a bunch of ugly thoughts like the ones I had in my head.

His room was cool. There were walk-out windows and a balcony on one side. The rain was still coming down. Everything was neat and dusted, from the wrinkleless bedcover to the long shiny bureau at the end of the bed. Papa went to the bureau and pointed to two photographs. One was of me and Mama. She was hugging me with her chin over my shoulder. The picture was taken by Papa who sat only inches from us. He took it when we were picnicking. It's all face and hair. My face. Mama's face. Our face. I looked just like Mama.

I realized that when I looked at the picture next to ours. It was of Mama when she went to school for the first time. Except for the tiny freckle under Mama's right eye, we could've been twins.

Papa sat down on the chair by the window and pulled me into his lap. I stared down at his feet. He was wearing those scruffy, old slippers that still smelled of pine because he kept them in the box of shavings Mama used to wrap them in. Seeing them made me smile.

Giving me a squeeze he said, "You're a lot like your mother, in all the good ways." He poked me in the tummy. "You're creative, loving, strong spirited. You and your mother are a pair."

"And I'm smart like you." I wanted to show him we belonged together, too.

He laughed, saying, "And truly honest like your mother."

I rested my head on Papa's shoulder and he kept talking. I could hear his voice echo in his chest. "You hear that rain, Nissa?" I hummed a yes. "Out there in that rain, Mama's thinking about us. Loving us."

"I hope so, Papa."

"I know so, Nissa." He hugged me. "I'm sorry for not saying it more often." Papa rubbed my back and before I could get two thoughts end to end to sort them out, I was asleep.

* * *

It was a feeling that woke me. It wasn't a sound. The rain was still coming down like chattering fairies. The house was quiet. There was no thunder. I was in Mama's bed, her pillow in my arms. It was getting dark, but the lamp by her bed was on. Inside, I felt a chilliness that doesn't come from being cold. It was a chill of excitement that gave me goose bumps on my head and made my hair sit up straight. I thought, so this is what a miracle felt like.

I knew Mama was back. Thank the Lord, my mama had come back. I ran to the window. Standing in the middle of the muddy street was my mama. She was in a yellow dress, her hair, straight and heavy with rain, draping down to just above her waist, her arms held out to the sky, her face wide with a smile, her teeth a glowing white in the evening shadows. Time skipped a beat. Everything held its breath, then I realized Mama was calling my name.

I wanted to jump out that window and fly down to her, but I ran through the front door instead. We were out in the rain, mud squishing between our toes as we ran toward each other. She caught me under the arms and swung me into the air, shouting, "My duchess!"

"Mama!" I was screaming it over and over.

Setting me down, she looked at me sideways. "You aren't mad at me?"

Wishing I had cherries to throw, I gave her a push. "You should be covered with mud!" I wasn't mad, but she deserved to end up in a mud puddle, maybe even worse.

"I should hang from a tent pole by my hair." She pulled at it.

"It's so long." I touched the wet strands. The last I'd see

her, it was only a few inches below her shoulders, but of course it was curly when it was dry.

"And you grew up." Her face looked a little twisted. If she wasn't soaking wet, I'd probably have seen her tears.

Mama threw her head back to take a drink of God's tap water. "Isn't this grand? Louisiana's going to slide right into the ocean? Good riddance!" She waved good-bye to the state.

"Mama." I wasn't so excited anymore. Thinking about her all those months made it easy to figure her out in a wink. "You just came to say good-bye."

Mama crouched down, so she was looking me in the eye, the hem of her dress draped into the mud. "I came to do what I should've done months ago." She held my arms. Her strong hands touched me and it felt like I got struck by lightning. "I came to say good-bye, for now. Just for now, honey."

"Why? Why, Mama?"

Mama gave a growling yell as she stood up. She took my hand, then led me into the house. "I don't see a reason to air our laundry in the street since people in this town seem to be so against it." We marched right through the house. In one door, out the other. On the way through, Mama held up a hand to Papa and Lara as they stood in the kitchen, their hands wet, sleeves rolled up, and towels over their shoulders, looking like they were watching a woman-sized hurricane waltz through the house. "Greetings to the happy couple." Mama said it like they were just a couple of townsfolk she knew by name.

We went out to the benches under the cherry tree and

sat down. It seemed so odd to have her so close. It was like she was my mama and a complete stranger all rolled into one. Under the branches, I only felt every other drop or so. It would've taken a thousand, million, trillion drops to make the muddled feeling inside me wash away.

"Mothers don't leave, Nissa." Mama said it as if she was talking about some other woman and she'd never do such a thing.

"Papa said nothing would change the fact that you're my mama."

"By blood, Nissa. By blood and the love I feel for you." She held me, but it felt more like Mary had her arm around me.

"Did you miss me, Mama?"

She started to rock as she wailed, "Oh, miss you? My heart's in pieces."

"Then why'd you leave?"

"You'd have to grow up before I could answer that question to your satisfaction, and neither one of us can afford to sit here and wait that long."

"Mrs. Carroll says I'm close to sixty inside my head, is that old enough?"

Mama rubbed my head. "You got water in there? Being old isn't a good thing for a child, Nissa. You see that's our problem. You've been more than half an adult from the moment you were born and I've never been more than half a child all my life."

"You trying to say you need to grow up and I need to grow down?" I asked the question and nearly laughed at myself it was so silly.

"Sounds about right."

I wasn't sure where that left us, so I asked, "You don't love Papa anymore?"

Mama stood up. "No, no, we're not going to play this game, Nissa. I've asked these questions of myself a thousand times and I don't have the answers. I don't have a reason for why I lost three of my children to death. I don't have an explanation for why I can't see myself sitting on a Louisiana front porch with Ivar Bergen in 1971. I have no idea why I can't make a friend in this Parish to save my life. Am I insane? No. Do I love you? Enough to absorb you into my soul. Am I a good mother? You tell me, Nissa."

I stared at her. There was no answer. My mind was vacant. Not a thought in it. I never knew that could really happen until that minute and it felt like I could float.

"You don't know the answer and neither do I. That's just it, Nissa. I searched for the answers here in Harper until I felt like I was disappearing. I ran off to find the answers and they kept scampering away because I was dragging my feet on account of the fact that I felt so heart-heavy bad about leaving you. Now, I'm going to hunt them down. I'm going to do this proper—say my good-byes, walk away with my head held high, and find the life I'm looking for."

"Why can't you find it here?"

Mama pointed at the back stoop. Lara and Papa were standing there hand in hand. "Look, Nissa, I lost what I had here. My marriage. Your trust. I need to start over like your father did."

"What about me?"

Mama kissed me. "You have everything you need,

Nissa. A family who loves you. It doesn't matter if I'm standing in that kitchen," she pointed to the window, "or on a boat to Mexico. I still love you. The difference this time is that no matter where I go, you'll know it. I won't abandon you again, Baby. You'll know where to find me. You say you need me and I'll be here."

I wanted to say I needed her now, but she put her finger to my lips. The rain drizzled into my mouth. "Don't you say it," she warned. "You may think it, but you don't need it. You've got a good woman there to take care of you."

"But she's not you."

Mama backed toward the gate. "And you can thank heaven for that. Two of us in one lifetime and your poor father's likely to have a heart attack. No, Nissa, Miss Lara Ross isn't me. She's got a few things on her side though. Like stability. You won't find her walking out of an empty house with a badly packed suitcase in hand."

"Don't go." I said it, but I knew she was already gone.

"If I stay, I'll lose what's left of my sanity. I go now or I'll never come back."

I tried to think of something to say. I had a million questions floating through my mind. What about the Sawdust Man? Where will you go, Mama? When will I see you? None of them reached my lips. I was instantly hopeless.

Mama was waving from the back gate when Grandma Dee shouted from an upstairs window, "And who will take care of you, Heirah Rae?"

"Lord knows, Mama!" she shouted back, waving real high so Grandma Dee could see. "You take damn good care of my baby girl, Miss Lara Ross, or I'll come hunting you!"

"Yes, ma'am," Lara called back.

I ran to the gate as Mama turned down the alley. She walked down the middle of the road without looking back. She never so much as turned her head to the side. She just kept right on walking.

The Death of the Sawdust Man

I STARTED WALKING RIGHT OFF AFTER MAMA. I DIDN'T EXPECT to catch up. I was just walking. Papa came into the alley after me. I heard him call my name, but then Miss Ross said, "Let her be."

If I didn't feel so hollow inside, I'd have thanked her for letting me go. I didn't want nobody nosy and mean hounding me, so I walked along the railroad tracks that ran along behind Tellah Street. The moon was up and full, so my way was all blue and clear, but my thoughts were all misty and small—things like there's a smashed penny on the rail, Mama's gone, and I've got a hole in my shoe. I heard Creole music dancing in the moist air like it was chasing away the rain. Creole's got a bit of power I love—like conjure music that can send away the rain and charge your soul happy with a fiddle bow. I found myself tipping this way and that on the rail to the beat of the music. I was even a bit happy dancing on my own.

Before I knew it, I was dipping and twirling right in front of the men on the back porch of the Crocked Gator. A group of men were sitting on the back porch drinking beer and pointing at me. I suppose they were talking before I showed up to make a fool out of myself. I was about to run when Otis Dupree held his bottle up to point at me, saying, "Ain't that Miss Heirah's girl?"

They knew my mama? I was glued to the spot. What did they know about her? From the doorway, Rinnie Lee said, "That's right. What you doing here at this time a night, Nissa?"

"Walking."

"Ira!" Otis bellowed and I thought for sure he could shout loud enough for Papa to hear him back at our place. Ira Simmons came to the door. Putting his arm around Rinnie Lee to give her a little squeeze, he said, "Whatya want, Otis?"

"You been looking for this child?" He pointed at me with his bottle again.

"Nissa." Mr. Simmons stumbled over Miss Rinnie Lee's feet to come toward me. The other men laughed and I had to bite my lip to keep from joining them. Mr. Simmons looked worried about something. I was afraid to even smile. "Did I hear your mama was in town?"

"She's gone." I was mad enough to spit fire. How did he know about Mama? Did everyone in town know her better than me?

"She left something with me and I don't want to be holding on to it no more. You think your papa can come get it?"

"What is it?"

"Show it to her!" Miss Rinnie Lee yelled. "It's for her anyhow."

"For me?" I asked Mr. Simmons.

"Why not," he said to Miss Rinnie Lee. Turning to me, he smiled, saying, "Come on down off those tracks and I'll show you."

He held my hand so I didn't fall and we walked behind the cafe to go to his shop two doors down. "So long, child!" Otis yelled from the porch. I waved good-bye, but I was thinking about what Mama could've left with Ira Simmons. I thought maybe she'd left the silver brush and mirror she promised to give to me, but there'd be no reason she'd give it to him.

The shop was dark when we went in. The sawdust was part of the air. I was coughing when Mr. Simmons lit the lantern. It took me a minute to catch my breath. He went to the corner where there was a hulk of a thing covered up with a canvas. He pulled the canvas off—it made a happy slithering sound as it slid across the surface of the object underneath. I saw shiny brown wood that was almost black.

"She made this," he said, smiling. "I showed her how. She's good at it, too."

Stepping up to the corner, I saw that it was a dresser. Not just any dresser though. It was Mama's. Each drawer was alive with flowers. I could run my fingers over the petals and leaves. Even the handles were hidden under ivy and roses. I opened a drawer and Mama had painted the insides with more blossoms—pink, blue, yellow; hibiscus, roses, bougainvillea. They were so pretty and real I felt I was falling into a garden just looking down into the drawer.

"Your birthday's coming up, isn't it?"

I couldn't talk. I was staring deep into that drawer

hoping Mama was somewhere in the garden I was seeing, planting and weeding, waiting for me to show up.

"You all right?"

I had to look away. I was crying already and it'd only get worse if I didn't turn away from those flowers. I stared at the floor. There was a carpet of sawdust. Sawdust! Mama was sneaking away to make me a dresser. There was no Sawdust Man. I started laughing. I even did a little dance step in that dirty old dust. "No more Sawdust Man," I sang to myself, smooshing the tiny wood chips around.

"Who are you talking about?" Mr. Simmons asked, laughing.

"Nobody!" I shouted. Mama had done it again. She'd fooled us all. There was no other man. There was just Mama and her tightly kept wings ready to fly. She was flying as I stood there—flying off to some great place where they didn't yell at you for stargazing on a roof, burning gardens, drinking hibiscus tea, or hanging underpants on a clothesline. I just wish I could've flown behind her.

"I've got to tell Papa!" I turned and ran out of there as if I had fire in my feet.

I was out of breath and rubbery when I got to our front porch. Lara was sitting on the swing by herself. "Where's Papa?"

She looked like she was thinking of crying when she said, "With your grandmother, looking for you."

I was mad at her for being so sad when I had just found out Mama had fooled everybody and built the best dresser ever. Then I realized Mama and I had tromped all over her wedding day. "I didn't mean to cause problems, Lara."

242 The Year of the Sawdust Man

Lara laughed. I thought she was making fun of me, but she said, "I know."

"I ruined your wedding day."

"It was a wonderful day." She nodded. "The night's been a little lonely though."

I went and sat next to her. "I'll keep you company until Papa comes back."

"All right." We stared at the other end of the porch for a bit, then she said, "What would you say to cooking something up for when they come back?"

"Man-shaped muffins!" I shouted.

She giggled. "Ivar told me about those." Standing up, she clapped her hands together. "Let's make muffin men!"

I jumped up and followed her. I helped her find everything she needed, then I watched her wartless hands flitting from here to there for sugar, eggs, milk—she was so quick it was like watching a hummingbird. "How about cinnamon?" she asked.

I nodded. I wasn't thinking about cinnamon. I was watching her standing in Mama's kitchen like it was her own. And it was. It was her kitchen, her house, her garden, her husband. At that moment, I realized, I was her daughter. When I wasn't paying attention, Lara Jean Ross Bergen became my day-to-day mama.

Mama had finally said her good-byes and given it all away. I knew she wasn't leaving me behind. She was taking me with her, or my love anyway. Lara was ready to step right in—weed Mama's garden, love Mama's husband, and care for Mama's daughter.

* * *

The Death of the Sawdust Man 243

Lying in bed that night, I tried to be happy. Everyone had what they wanted. Papa and Lara had each other. Grandma Dee and I knew Mama was okay. Mama had her freedom, but I kept imagining her walking right off the edge of the earth. If she wasn't right there beside me, it seemed like Mama couldn't quite *be* at all. As Papa tucked me in, I remembered what he had said and knew Mama was somewhere in the darkness outside my window, loving me.

A Normal Life

IT WAS MY BIRTHDAY A WEEK AFTER MAMA LEFT. I WAS TWELVE that year and ready for hair curls. The only problem was, Mama wasn't there to show me how to curl my hair. I sat at her vanity table drawing circles in the place where her curling iron used to sit. Grandma Dee had packed it away. I'd probably never see it again. Papa had been talking about sending all her things when she called to tell where she was at. He always said "when," but I was thinking "if."

I was about to cry when I heard Lara call out, "Nissa!" It seemed so odd to suddenly have a woman calling out my name early in the morning when there's no noise in the street and the sound of a voice can echo off the walls. A mother's voice echoes like that.

I was afraid to go downstairs. I thought it meant admitting to everyone in the house that I'd accepted Lara as my new mother. Papa tapped on the door and scared me. "Breakfast."

I opened the door and he was walking downstairs while putting his tie on. It seemed like such a normal, ordinary thing to do and I realized I hadn't felt normal or ordinary for a long, long time. Since the day Mama had left for the first time, I guess. Could be that's what everyone was fussing about with everyone telling me I was so grown-up. Thinking about happier things like grub hunting and playing jacks sure beat wondering if my mama would ever come back.

When I got to the kitchen, Lara was putting ham cutlets on the plates. She moved around the kitchen like she'd been there when they built it. Maybe Mama was right. Miss Ross could be the type of day-to-day mama who would always be there when I got up in the morning.

Where'd that leave my mama. In the wind, I guess. Mama would always be in the wind, her love for me blowing in with the breeze. It hurt to think we'd never be together again, but something inside me said that wasn't true. I'd like to think it was God, seeing me and Mama and where we'd be in days to come. He knew there'd be times for us again. She said I could find her when I needed her, but she hadn't called to say where she was. Papa said she would and Papa didn't lie.

I smiled, thinking how I'd be able to pack my bags and go off to some distant place and be in Mama's house. Maybe in New Orleans where she'd be learning how to dance professionally at Marie Fontaine's School of Dance. I could help her paint murals and plant flowers. Me and Mama were still a we and would be forever, if she called.

The squirt of an orange woke me out of my dreaming. Grandma Dee was squeezing out the last bit of juice. Papa took his seat and I slid into my chair.

"Morning, Sweetie," Grandma Dee said as she gave me a glass of juice.

"Morning," I said.

"You like brown sugar on your ham?" Lara asked, tapping the jar of brown sugar on the table with a fork.

"Sure," I told her.

Lara put the pan back on the stove, then they both sat down. I looked around the table at the white plates, the clear glasses filled with foamy fresh juice, the ham curled up and brown at the edges, the salt and pepper shakers coated with their spices, the knives lying crooked next to the plates, and the napkins folded up under the forks. It was as normal as normal can be. I felt all fluttery special inside.

I almost wished it wasn't my birthday so the day could be normal from start to finish. That wouldn't be so hard to do. Papa always pretended it wasn't my birthday until the minute I was really born, then we'd sing "Happy Birthday" at the top of our lungs. Mama'd bring out the cake she'd baked and Papa would get the presents. Papa had brought home the dresser days before, so it didn't seem like a real gift. Oh, I loved it. I'd keep it polished and pretty forever, but it wasn't an unwrapping type gift—it was more like a hidden treasure.

What's more, I wouldn't get to eat one of Mama's cakes. I was feeling kind of sad when Grandma Dee said, "I'm taking the train back to Mississippi tomorrow."

"Really?" Papa raised his eyebrows.

He didn't say much. He didn't want her to get embarrassed and change her mind. Grandma Dee had a lot of strong thoughts, but she seldom told people what she was thinking. To tell the truth, she might reconsider her own name if she thought someone would doubt it was hers.

I held my breath, waiting for Grandma Dee to say how she felt about Mama's leaving again. She picked up her knife and fork, then said, "Can't see myself explaining all this to Jared over a telephone. He'll have plenty of questions. Don't you worry now, Nissa. I'll be back so often you'll wish me dead."

Papa and I smiled. We knew she was just kidding about the dying part.

Grandma added, "Won't nothing keep me from being your grandma."

I looked at Papa, then noticed Lara was smiling, too. She knew it was a good thing for me to see Grandma Dee. The width of Lara's smile, the way her eyes looked a little brighter, said she really cared about me. That made it a whole lot easier to like her.

I was about to cut into my ham when someone knocked at the back door.

"I'll get it!" I yelled, running for the back door without putting my silverware down. I knew it had to be Mary. She was the only one, besides Mr. Rainey, who used the back door.

I was surprised to see Mrs. Carroll standing on the other side of the screen door. She pointed at the knife I still held in my hand. "What's that for?"

I laughed in embarrassment. Putting the silverware into my pockets, I told her, "We're having breakfast."

"Oh, terribly sorry." Mrs. Carroll tipped her head forward in apology. "We'll come back later."

"No, no," Papa said from the kitchen doorway. "Come in. Nissa would love to see Mary."

"If you're sure, then I'll step aside for Mary's surprise."

Mrs. Carroll stepped over to reveal Mary who was standing on a flagstone, holding a cake.

"I made it myself," Mary shouted. Her cake looked delicious. The pink frosting was perfectly rippled and the cake wasn't the least bit lopsided like mine always were. In fact, Mary's cake looked as good as her mother's. Mary said, "It's chocolate with cherry frosting."

"Great!" I yelled. "Thank you!"

Mrs. Carroll said, "We all wish you have a Happy Birthday, Nissa."

Mary smiled, saying, "Even Teddy."

"Mary," Mrs. Carroll frowned. Mary just looked at me and shrugged.

Papa stepped in front of me to open the door. "Thank you, both," he said as he leaned forward and took the cake from Mary. He asked the Carrolls, "Would the two of you like a slice now?"

"Oh, no." Mrs. Carroll waved the idea away as I slipped past Papa.

"Thank you, Mary." I gave her a hug.

"It was no problem. Happy Birthday," Mary said as Papa continued to try to get Mrs. Carroll to come in. Mary whispered, "Did you really see your ma?"

"Yes," I nodded, smiling.

"People are saying she went crazy."

I kind of wished Mary was still holding the cake so I could've smooshed it into her face. "Well, your mama's afraid of cats!"

"Girls." Mrs. Carroll turned to us with a frown on her face.

"Sorry," Mary and I said in unison.

"We better go now, Mary." Mrs. Carroll stepped off the back steps, saying, "You have a nice birthday now, Nissa."

"Thank you, Mrs. Carroll," I said.

Mary gave me a strangling hug as she whispered, "Pals forever, no matter what our mothers do or say."

I stared back at her as Mrs. Carroll shouted from the back gate, "Come along, Mary!"

"Right?" Mary asked.

"Forever." I smiled.

She waved good-bye, then followed her mother into the alley. Papa came to stand next to me. "That was pretty nice of her." He touched my shoulder. "And this cake looks great!"

"Sure does." I nodded, then led the way back into the house.

"Shall we skip to dessert?" Papa asked as he set the cake down in the center of the table.

"Ivar!" Lara gave Papa a little push.

"How silly," said Grandma Dee.

Seeing as how Mary's cake had to be the next best thing to a cake Mama made, I said, "I like the idea."

"All right." Papa went to the knife rack, but someone knocked on the front door before he could get a knife. "Wonder who that could be?" he asked, walking out of the room. "I'll be right back."

Papa went to get the door. I heard him say hello, but I couldn't hear the visitor's voice. For a second, I was sure it was Mama coming home to wish me a happy birthday. I ran into the hallway ready to see Mama, light on her feet in a pretty new purple dress. But it was Mr. Minkie stooped over and sweaty in his bow tie and grocer's apron.

"You have a phone call, Nissa," he told me.

"Really?" I said, running for the door.

Papa caught me by the shoulders as I passed in front of him. He leaned down to whisper, "Maybe it's a birthday call."

I laughed at Papa's sideways birthday wish. "I'll be back!" I shouted, pulling away, then running across the street, leaving Mr. Minkie on our porch.

I was out of breath when I reached the phone booth. So I panted into the receiver, trying to get enough air to say hello.

"Are you dying?" Mama asked from the other end.

"Mama!"

"You ran, did you? Does that mean you miss me?"

"More than anything!"

She laughed. "I was just thinking, maybe I could come down this weekend and give you a birthday present."

"Where are you now?"

"I'm in Tennessee for a bit. On my way to Chicago."

"Chicago!" I couldn't imagine Mama in the freezing hustle and noise of a big old city up North.

"Going to the birthplace of my roses, Nissa."

"Why?" I was shouting worse than Grandma Dee.

"Why? Why? Why? When will you ever learn to let things be."

"When I grow down I guess," I laughed.

Mama faked a laugh to say "not so funny" without speaking. "How about my birthday present?"

"I'd love to see you."

"Would you love stars on your ceiling? I have the paints here. I could paint the night sky on your ceiling."

"Like the flowers in the dresser?"

"Dresser?"

"The dresser you made with Ira Simmons."

"You know about that?" She sounded mad.

"Yes."

"That's your hope chest, Nissa. You weren't supposed to have that until you were sixteen."

"Did you ever plan on coming back?"

"Not when I left."

We didn't speak for a minute. I was mad at Mama for thinking about leaving me forever and she was mad at me for getting my coming-out gift early. Then Mama said, "What's done is done. I want to paint you a night sky."

"Can you make it sort of purple so I can see your roses in the stars?"

Mama was silent for a moment. I thought maybe she didn't remember the night when we'd looked at the purple color in the night sky from the roof of our porch, then she said, "I love you, Nissa."

"I love you, too, Mama."

"That'll be one purply night sky I'm going to paint, Nissa. You just wait and see, my birthday girl."

I giggled. "I'll love it, Mama."

"I know you will."

Right there, right then, Mama felt close enough to touch. I had my mama back. I had it all—Mama, Papa, Grandma Dee, Grandpa Jared, Mary Carroll, and maybe even Lara.